The Spy Who Loved Me: A Scarlet Swanson Story

By Diane Wyatt

Copyright © 2025 Diane Wyatt
Published by

TABLE OF CONTENTS

Part I: The Making of a Spy

Part II: Love in the Line of Fire

Part III: The Final Mission

Part I: The Making of a Spy

Prologue: A Life in the Shadows

The cold bit at Scarlet Swanson's cheeks as she sprinted through the darkness, her breath coming in ragged gasps. The forest around her blurred—a tangle of blackened trees, moonlit snow, and the echo of boots pounding behind. Branches clawed at her arms as if the night itself wanted to hold her back.

Ahead, Boris didn't slow down. He didn't have to look back to know she was right behind him; he trusted her, and she trusted him—more than she should.

A burst of gunfire shattered the silence behind them, the sharp cracks chasing them like ghosts through the trees. Scarlet ducked instinctively, her pulse hammering in her ears, louder than the shots, louder than the fear. Her legs burned, her lungs screamed, but she kept going. There was no stopping now. Not when freedom was so close. Not when lives—their lives—hung in the balance.

"Down!" Boris hissed, grabbing her wrist and yanking her behind a snow-covered boulder. They dropped low, hearts racing in sync, their bodies pressed together in the dirt and frost. The roar of an engine cut through the air—jeeps, headlights slicing the dark. Too close.

Scarlet turned her head toward him. Even in the shadows, his eyes were steady. Calm. His hand, warm despite the cold, brushed her cheek in a fleeting, human moment that had no place in war—but they didn't care. They weren't just spies tonight. They were survivors.

"Ten seconds," he murmured, voice low, accent heavy with tension. "Then we run."

Scarlet nodded, her chest tight—not just from exertion, but from the weight of everything unsaid between them. Ten seconds could mean life or death. But all she could think about was him.

The world shrank to a countdown in her head.

Ten… The memory of their first mission together—an opulent ballroom, the scent of champagne, his eyes meeting hers across a sea of strangers.

Nine… The first time she realized she wasn't pretending anymore. She didn't just trust him. She needed him.

Eight… The night they kissed, knowing it could cost them everything.

Seven… A shot rang out. She flinched. Boris didn't.

Six… He touched her hand. "Stay with me," he said.

Five… She blinked against the sting in her eyes, against the wind and the fear.

Four… "I'm not leaving you," she whispered.

Three…

Two…

One…

They ran.

No more hesitation. No more regrets. Just two people, fleeing the only world they had ever known, risking it all for a chance at something more - something real.

As they crossed the ridge and the first light of dawn touched the horizon, Scarlet stumbled, fell to her knees, and laughed—a breathless, delirious sound. They'd made it. For now.

Boris helped her up, and for a moment, they simply stood there, side by side, staring into the pale morning sky.

"You okay?" he asked, his voice rough.

Scarlet nodded, eyes still on the rising sun. "Ask me when this is over."

He smiled—small, tired, but real. "It'll never be over."

She turned to him, her heart pounding with something beyond fear now. "Then I guess I'll just have to live with it."

He pulled her close, pressing his forehead to hers. "We both will."

In the distance, the world they left behind burned. But in each other's arms, Scarlet and Boris didn't feel like fugitives. They felt alive.

And for the first time, Scarlet understood what it truly meant to live in the shadows—and to love in them, too.

Chapter 1: The Assignment

Scarlet Swanson stood at the top of the marble staircase, her heart beating a slow, steady rhythm beneath the soft silk of her evening gown. Below her, the grand ballroom was a spectacle of wealth and diplomacy — glittering chandeliers cast golden light over a crowd of political elite, military brass, and the type of men who wore secrets as easily as they wore tailored suits.

She inhaled deeply, squaring her shoulders as she descended into the throng. Each step was deliberate. Calculated. Trained. Her heels clicked softly against polished stone, the sound swallowed by the swell of a string quartet playing something elegant and old. She looked like she belonged. That was the key.

Tonight, Scarlet wasn't just attending a diplomatic gala. She was hunting.

She'd spent weeks preparing for this moment — memorizing names, titles, international alliances, cover stories. She was "Sophia Blake" tonight, an attaché with the U.S. State Department, here on assignment to observe and report. The reality? Scarlet's real job was much darker: extract sensitive information from a suspected foreign agent — codename **Viper** — and disappear without a trace.

Her emerald eyes scanned the room, noting exits, security placements, and the subtle tension of guarded conversations. Men in tuxedos spoke in clipped tones. Women glittered like ornaments on a

Christmas tree. And somewhere in this sea of polished civility was the man who might be holding documents that could trigger an international crisis.

Scarlet moved through the crowd like smoke — smiling, nodding, making polite conversation, but never stopping too long. Her training had taught her to blend in, to draw just enough attention without arousing suspicion. She was the kind of woman men noticed, but never quite remembered. That, too, was intentional.

Her dress — a deep emerald green that matched her eyes — hugged her body in all the right places, catching the light and, occasionally, the gaze of passing diplomats. She accepted a flute of champagne from a waiter, raising it to her lips without taking a sip.

"Miss Blake, isn't it?" a voice said behind her — smooth, cultured, and laced with curiosity.

Scarlet turned, the corners of her mouth lifting into a perfect smile. This was him. Viper.

The man was tall, impeccably dressed in a black tuxedo that fit him like a second skin. His hair was dark, slicked back with precision, and his eyes — a piercing steel gray — held a glimmer of both amusement and danger.

"Guilty," Scarlet replied, offering her hand. "And you are?"

"Victor Drakov," he said, taking her hand with a gentle but firm grip. "Energy sector liaison. Eastern European trade delegation."

Scarlet's heart skipped a beat. Not from surprise, but from recognition. **Victor Drakov** was Viper — a known operative working under the cover of economic diplomacy. He was here for more than trade talks.

"Well, Mr. Drakov," she said, eyes never leaving his. "Are you enjoying the event?"

"Only now," he replied, a smile playing on his lips. "You stand out."

She laughed softly, tilting her head. "In a room like this, standing out isn't always safe."

His smile widened, as if he appreciated the subtle warning. "Ah, but danger makes things interesting, doesn't it?"

Scarlet's pulse quickened. This was no casual flirtation. Every word was measured, every glance deliberate. She was being tested, just as she was testing him.

As they spoke, Scarlet subtly guided the conversation — steering it toward geopolitics, trade imbalances, and security protocols. She needed to bait him, to make him comfortable, and then draw out the information her agency so desperately needed.

"You must get tired of these events," she said, eyes glancing around the room. "So much posturing, so little substance."

"True," he replied, sipping his drink. "But sometimes, hidden among the empty chatter, are conversations that change the world."

Scarlet smiled, feeling the first crack in his armor. "Would you care for some air?"

Victor hesitated for only a moment before nodding. "Lead the way."

She guided him toward the terrace doors, her movements slow and poised. The cool night air swept over them as they stepped into the garden, the distant murmur of the party fading behind them.

The garden was quiet, illuminated by soft lights strung through ancient oaks and manicured hedges. The scent of roses lingered in the air, mixing with the faint trace of his cologne — something sharp, clean, with a hint of smoke.

Scarlet paused near a stone bench, turning to face him. "It's peaceful out here."

"Peace is rare in our world," Victor said, his eyes studying her. "You strike me as someone who understands that."

Scarlet met his gaze, letting a beat of silence pass. "Maybe."

He stepped closer, his presence commanding. There was an intensity in his eyes now, a flicker of suspicion — or perhaps interest. Scarlet couldn't tell which.

"Tell me, Sophia," he said, voice low. "Why are you really here tonight?"

Scarlet's heart hammered, but her expression didn't falter. She smiled, tilting her head slightly. "Same as you. To observe. To learn. And maybe to leave with something valuable."

Victor's eyes narrowed, not in anger, but in intrigue. He reached into his jacket — slowly — and pulled out a cigarette case. "You don't smoke," he said, almost as a statement.

Scarlet's smile widened. "How do you know?"

"Because I've been watching you," he said, lighting the cigarette. "And you watch the room like a hawk."

Her breath caught, but she didn't let it show. "Is that a compliment or a warning?"

He exhaled a plume of smoke into the night. "It's both."

Scarlet stepped closer, just enough to blur the lines between seduction and strategy. "I'd say the same about you."

For a moment, the air between them was electric — charged with tension and unspoken truths. Scarlet reached into her clutch, her fingers brushing the small recording device hidden inside. She had to push further, to get him to talk, to let something slip.

"Tell me something, Victor," she said softly, "do you believe in loyalty?"

His eyes darkened, just slightly. "To what?"

"To people. To causes. To countries."

Victor studied her, the cigarette forgotten in his hand. "Loyalty is a currency," he said at last. "And like all currencies, it can be bought, sold... or stolen."

Scarlet's stomach clenched. That was it. That was the opening.

She moved closer still, her voice barely above a whisper. "And what about trust?"

He didn't answer immediately. Instead, he reached out, brushing a strand of hair from her cheek. The touch was gentle — intimate — but there was a weight to it. A challenge.

"Trust is dangerous," he said. "Especially in our line of work."

Scarlet's breath caught; the truth laid bare in his words. He knew. Maybe not everything, but enough.

She had to end it — now.

"Well," she said, stepping back, "thank you for the conversation. I should return."

Victor's hand caught hers, not forcefully, but with intent. "You're not who you say you are."

Scarlet froze.

"I don't care," he added, voice low. "But be careful. Not everyone here is as forgiving."

He released her hand, letting her go. Scarlet turned without another word, her mind racing.

Back inside the ballroom, she moved quickly, locating her handler — a man posing as a server near the far wall. She gave the signal. Mission complete. The recording device had captured everything.

As she exited the event minutes later, stepping into the waiting car, Scarlet's hands trembled slightly in her lap.

Victor Drakov — Viper — had been more than a mark. There was something about him, something unsettling. He'd seen through her, and yet he hadn't turned her in.

As the car pulled away, Scarlet glanced back at the grand estate, its lights fading into the distance.

This mission was over. But something told her it wouldn't be the last time she saw him.

And she wasn't sure if that excited her or terrified her more.

As the car turned onto the main road, Scarlet leaned her head back against the cool leather seat, her eyes closing for just a moment. The hum of the engine, the faint scent of perfume and gun oil lingering on her skin, the muted city lights flashing past — it all felt surreal, as if she were drifting somewhere between the world of the living and the shadowed realm where spies like her truly existed. No one out there, in the real world, knew the kind of life she led. And maybe that was the point.

Victor Drakov — Viper — had unnerved her. Not because he had discovered her cover, but because he hadn't used it against her. That was what disturbed her most. He'd looked her straight in the eye, stripped away her alias with nothing but a few pointed words, and then let her walk away. That kind of move wasn't just rare — it was dangerous. It meant he was playing a longer game, and now she was part of it.

She rubbed her fingers together absently, the memory of his touch still warm against her skin. Too familiar. Too real. Scarlet had trained for years to keep herself distant — to see her marks as marks, nothing more. But Viper had blurred that line effortlessly, like a man who knew exactly how to unnerve someone without laying a finger on them — and then he'd done that, too.

Her phone buzzed once in her clutch — a coded message from her handler confirming the recording was clean and the extraction successful. That should have given her a sense of accomplishment.

Instead, all she felt was a dull ache in her chest, the kind that came from a question left unanswered — or worse, a door left open.

She exhaled slowly, forcing her thoughts to settle. Emotions were liabilities. Connections, distractions. She knew this. She believed it. Yet something about Viper — his gaze, the way he saw through her — had left a mark. It wasn't attraction, not exactly. It was recognition. Like they had both lived too long in the shadows and finally stumbled upon someone who knew what that darkness cost.

Scarlet's fingers drifted to the pendant around her neck, the one thing she wore from her real life, the one she tried not to think about. Her father had given it to her once. Before he disappeared. Before she learned that secrets ran in her blood. Her decision to join the agency had been driven by more than patriotism — it had been about answers. Closure. And the sense that somewhere in this world of espionage, she could find meaning in the lies.

The city skyline came into view — lights shimmering across the river like scattered stars. Somewhere out there, Victor Drakov was likely reviewing the same night from a very different angle. Had he let her go because he saw no threat? Or because he wanted her to feel indebted? Worse, was he laying a trap — luring her back into his orbit, knowing she would have no choice but to return?

Scarlet hated not knowing. Control was her armor. Precision was her shield. But tonight, both had cracked — and it wasn't just the mission that had pushed her to the edge. It was the look in his eyes when he touched her face, the way he spoke about trust like it was a game they both knew they couldn't win.

The car slowed in front of her building, a sleek high-rise with mirrored glass windows and guards who knew better than to ask questions. She stepped out, her heels clicking against the pavement, and nodded once to the doorman before disappearing into the elevator. As the doors closed, she caught her reflection in the mirror — poised, beautiful, dangerous. A woman who had everything under control.

And yet, as the elevator climbed floor after floor in silence, Scarlet's thoughts returned to Viper's words. *"You're not who you say you are."* Neither was he. But maybe, for the first time, she wasn't sure if that made them enemies... or something far more complicated.

Chapter 2: The Dance of Deception

Scarlet Swanson lived for moments like this — the edge of danger, the flicker of anticipation, the knowledge that one wrong move could shatter everything. The ballroom was her stage, the people her audience, and tonight, she played the role of the alluring, mysterious diplomat with perfection honed by years of training.

She had eyes on him now. Victor Drakov. Viper. Standing at the bar, his posture relaxed, the crystal tumbler in his hand catching the light as if it were part of his performance. He was magnetic in the way all dangerous men were — confident, unreadable, utterly aware of the power he held in any room.

Scarlet didn't let herself hesitate. Hesitation was weakness. She adjusted her stride — elegant but sure — her heels clicking softly against the polished floor, her dress catching the glow of the chandeliers overhead. She approached him not as prey, but as a rival.

He noticed her long before she reached him. Of course, he did.

"Ms. Blake," he said smoothly, turning to face her fully. "Back so soon?"

Her cover held — Sophia Blake, State Department attaché, here to observe and mingle. But they both knew it was a façade.

"I was curious," she replied with a small smile, accepting the drink the bartender offered her — champagne, un-sipped. "You're not easy to read."

Victor chuckled, the sound low and warm. "That's intentional."

Scarlet allowed a pause — the kind that hinted at interest, but never too much. "Do you prefer to watch from a distance or be part of the action?"

"That depends on who's offering the invitation." His eyes never left hers.

Scarlet's heart beat a fraction faster, but her smile never faltered. This was the dance of deception — words layered with meaning, glances that could mean everything or nothing, and a tension thick enough to feel in her bones.

She leaned against the bar, angling her body slightly toward him. "And if I asked you to take a walk? Somewhere a little less crowded?"

Another pause — deliberate, weighted. Then, he smiled, slow and deliberate. "Lead the way."

The garden beyond the ballroom was quiet, lit by delicate strings of lights woven through archways and trees. The scent of roses lingered in the air, mingling with the crisp night breeze. Scarlet led him along the stone path, her every step measured, her mind already cataloging every angle — every potential threat.

Viper walked beside her, hands in his pockets, his presence far too calm for a man under scrutiny. He wasn't just confident. He was comfortable with danger. That made him unpredictable.

"You don't strike me as someone who likes crowds," she said, glancing sideways at him.

He raised an eyebrow. "And yet you found me there."

"I'm good at finding things." She let the words hang in the air, watching his reaction.

Victor stopped walking, turning to face her fully. The light caught his features — sharp, chiseled, effortlessly attractive — but it was his eyes that held her. Cold steel, full of secrets.

"What are you looking for, Ms. Blake?"

There it was. The challenge.

Scarlet tilted her head, stepping closer, her voice barely above a whisper. "Answers."

A flicker of something crossed his face — amusement? Suspicion? She couldn't tell. That was the problem. Viper wasn't like the other marks. He didn't posture. He didn't overplay his hand. He simply watched, waited, and reacted. Like a predator.

He pulled a cigarette from his coat pocket, lighting it with a flick of silver. The smoke curled between them like a veil.

"You know, in my world, people who ask too many questions rarely get the answers they want."

Scarlet met his gaze without flinching. "And in mine, people who give the right answers get remembered."

Silence stretched between them, heavily, charged.

Then, he smiled. Not the polite smile of a diplomat. A real one. "You're dangerous."

She smiled back, slow and unapologetic. "So are you."

Victor took a drag from the cigarette, exhaling slowly. "Tell me something, Sophia. Are you here because you want something from me... or because you're curious?"

Scarlet's pulse quickened. She wasn't sure anymore.

Both.

"Can't it be both?" she asked.

For a moment, something shifted in his expression — a flicker of genuine interest. Then, as quickly as it came, it vanished.

"You're clever," he said, dropping the cigarette and crushing it underfoot. "But clever can get you killed."

Scarlet stepped closer, now only inches away. She could feel the heat radiating off him, smell the faint hint of cologne beneath the smoke. Her voice lowered, silk-wrapped steel.

"So can trust."

Victor studied her, his eyes narrowing just slightly.

"You're not who you say you are."

The words cut through the air like a blade, soft but deadly.

Scarlet's body tensed — her training screaming at her to retreat, to pivot — but her face remained composed. She met his gaze, letting silence answer for her.

And then... he did the unexpected.

He reached out, gently touching her face, his fingers lingering for just a second too long. Not an attack. A message.

"Be careful, Ms. Blake. Not everyone here is as forgiving as I am."

Her breath caught in her throat, but she refused to step back.

"I'll take my chances."

Victor smiled again — slow, calculated — and stepped away. "I hope so. Because I have a feeling we'll be seeing more of each other."

With that, he turned and disappeared into the shadows of the garden, leaving Scarlet alone under the lights, heart pounding, mind racing.

As she returned to the ballroom, the noise hit her like a wave — laughter, music, clinking glasses — as if nothing had happened. As if she hadn't just danced with danger and lived to tell the tale.

She crossed the room, eyes scanning for her handler — Agent Sloan, stationed near the exit, posing as a guest. Their eyes met, and Scarlet gave the subtlest nod. Mission complete. She had everything they needed — and more questions than answers.

Later, in the car, Scarlet sat in silence, her hands still tingling from Victor's touch, her thoughts clouded by his words.

"You're not who you say you are."

Neither was he.

And that scared her more than anything.

Because the dance of deception wasn't just about outwitting your opponent.

Sometimes... it was about not losing yourself in the process.

She stared out the window as the city lights blurred into streaks of gold and red, her reflection staring back at her — flawless, poised, unreadable. The mask she wore in public had become so second nature that sometimes she wasn't sure where it ended and she began. Beneath the elegant dress, the trained smile, and the carefully crafted lies, there was still a woman — one who felt too much, too deeply, for a profession that demanded nothing but detachment.

Victor Drakov had shaken something loose in her. Not just because he'd seen through her cover, but because he'd seen *her*. Not the agent, not the persona — the woman behind it. And in that split-second when his fingers had brushed her face, it wasn't fear she'd felt. It was heat. Recognition. A flash of something dangerous that no training could prepare her for: connection.

Scarlet hated it. She hated that he lingered in her thoughts, that his voice replayed in her mind like a song she couldn't shake. It was reckless. Unprofessional. And yet, somewhere deep inside, she knew this wouldn't be the last time their paths crossed. Drakov hadn't played all his cards — and neither had she. There was something building between them, a tension that felt less like a game and more like a fuse waiting to be lit.

Her phone buzzed in her lap — a secure message from her handler. Debrief at 0700. No delay. Scarlet locked the screen without replying. She wasn't ready to talk about the night, not yet. Not when the mission had veered so far off script. She'd gotten what they needed — intelligence, confirmation of Viper's presence, the beginnings of a trail — but what she hadn't counted on was the storm he'd stirred inside her.

As the car slowed in front of her building, Scarlet took a breath and steeled herself. This life — the secrets, the danger, the endless web of manipulation — demanded everything. And the only way to survive it was to stay sharp, stay guarded, and never let anyone too close. But as she stepped into the lobby and rode the elevator to her floor, she couldn't shake the feeling that Victor Drakov had already slipped past every defense she thought she had — and that terrified her more than any mission ever could.

And that terrified her more than any mission ever could.

Because missions were black and white — success or failure, live or die. There was structure, protocol, and a clean set of rules hidden beneath layers of chaos. But what she felt now wasn't part of any mission. It was messy, unpredictable, and real — and it was starting to seep through the cracks she'd spent years fortifying. Scarlet had faced men with guns, terrorists with detonators, and agents who'd sold their souls for power. But this? This was something she couldn't shoot her way out of.

She stepped into her apartment, locking the door behind her with a quiet click. The silence inside was oppressive, pressing in from all sides. No voices. No orders. Just her heartbeat — too fast, too loud — and the echo of Drakov's words still dancing in her head. *"You're not who you say you are."* He wasn't wrong. She hadn't been Scarlet Swanson in that garden; she'd been someone else entirely — a woman caught between duty and desire, between fear and fascination.

Stripping off her dress, she let it fall in a pool of silk at her feet. She stood in front of the mirror, staring at her reflection — the faint bruises on her arms from the recoil of a weapon, the delicate lines around her eyes that no makeup could fully erase, the small pendant at her throat that didn't belong to the mission but to the girl she used to be. Who was she, really, beneath the layers of deception and control? And what would be left if she let them slip?

Scarlet wasn't supposed to care. That was rule number one. The moment you cared, you compromised — yourself, the mission, the agency. But somehow, Victor Drakov had slipped past every firewall in her mind. He hadn't threatened her. He hadn't needed to. He'd simply looked at her like he knew her, and for the first time in years, she'd felt seen — and it had shaken her to her core.

She poured herself a drink — neat, no ice — and stood at the window, staring at the city below. Lights flickered like stars trapped in steel and glass, millions of lives playing out in ignorance of the war that was always brewing beneath their feet. They lived in a world of simple truths. She didn't. Her world was shadow and smoke, loyalty and betrayal — and now, something personal was threatening to unravel it all.

What if he was playing her? No — of course he was playing her. That was the only way to survive in their line of work. And yet... the way he'd touched her face, the way he'd warned her to be careful — there'd been something in his eyes. Not calculation. Not coldness.

Something else. Recognition, maybe. Or regret. And that was even more dangerous. Because Scarlet didn't know what to do with a man like that.

She couldn't afford to be distracted. Not now. Not with Blackthorn missions surfacing again — the kind of operations that never saw the light of day, the kind that broke agents without ever firing a bullet. And if Viper was part of that world — as her gut told her he was — then getting close to him wasn't just risky. It was suicide.

Still, as the night wore on and the city began to sleep, Scarlet didn't. She lay awake, the sheets tangled around her legs, her thoughts a blur of what-ifs and memories. The way his voice dropped when he'd said her name. The way he watched her like a man who understood exactly what it cost to live in the shadows. And the way, just for a second, she hadn't wanted to run from him... but toward him.

Scarlet Swanson had survived missions that left seasoned agents broken. She'd outwitted criminals, infiltrated governments, and walked away from explosions with nothing but scars and a file stamped "confidential." But the look in Viper's eyes had undone her in ways she hadn't expected. It had stripped her bare without ever touching skin. It had made her remember what it felt like to want something not because of duty — but because of choice.

And choice, in her world, was a dangerous illusion. One that could cost her everything.

Tomorrow, she would wear the mask again — slip into the role, follow the mission, and play her part. But tonight, in the silence, Scarlet faced the truth she didn't want to admit: Victor Drakov had become more than a target. He was a threat — not to the agency, not to the mission... but to her heart. And no amount of training had prepared her for that.

Chapter 3: Crossing Lines

The meeting room was colder than it needed to be. Not from air conditioning, but from the kind of chill that came with top-secret briefings, the kind where everyone in the room knew something was about to go very, very wrong.

Scarlet sat near the end of the long black conference table, hands folded, eyes sharp. Across from her, the Director paced slowly, a file in one hand and a mug of burnt coffee in the other. A digital map of Eastern Europe glowed on the wall behind him — cities illuminated, borders highlighted, red zones pulsing like pressure points.

A low voice broke the silence.

"She's ready."

Scarlet turned slightly at the sound.

That was the first time she saw him — not just passed in a hallway or glimpsed in a dossier — but *really* saw him. Boris Volkov. The agency's most senior field asset in the Eastern Corridor. Ex-military intelligence. Tactical specialist. Cold War relic reborn in a digital age. And now, apparently, her partner.

He stood tall, arms folded, dark suit slightly rumpled but still authoritative. Everything about him was sharp — jawline, eyes, tone.

But it wasn't arrogance. It was control. The kind that came from decades of watching men lie, bleed, and vanish.

He glanced at her once — just once — and in that look, she felt it.

Recognition. Assessment. Caution. And something else. Something unspoken.

Scarlet sat straighter.

The Director dropped the file on the table with a thud.

"Operation Blackthorn just escalated. You'll both be flying out within the next twenty-four hours. Noofficial cover. No agency support once you cross into Belarus."

"Target?" Boris asked, voice low and clipped.

"Intel leak," the Director replied. "We believe someone inside the regional diplomatic council is passing information to Victor Drakov."

Scarlet didn't flinch. The name still struck a chord in her chest, but she kept her expression neutral.

"Drakov again?" Boris's voice held something just under the surface. Not fear. Not anger. Memory.

Scarlet didn't ask.

"He's not our objective. Yet," the Director said. "You're to identify the leak, intercept the documents, and neutralize the source. Discretion is key."

Boris glanced sideways at Scarlet. "She's green."

Scarlet didn't blink. "I'm ready."

Their eyes locked — neither backing down.

The Director exhaled slowly. "You'll brief her. You leave together. You return together. Understood?"

Boris nodded once.

Scarlet did the same.

But they both knew nothing in their line of work ever went that cleanly.

Later, in the training facility's briefing sublevel, Scarlet leaned against the wall, arms crossed, watching Boris pace in front of the projection screen. He was going over extraction routes, code protocols, embassy safe zones. His voice was measured, accented slightly — Russian, but eroded by years of English.

She let him speak for a while before finally saying, "You don't think I'm capable."

Boris looked up. "I think you're smart. Controlled. And you look like you belong in any room you enter. That's half the job."

She tilted her head. "And the other half?"

He met her gaze. "Knowing when not to speak."

Scarlet's mouth twitched into the hint of a smile. "Duly noted."

Boris stepped closer, lowering his voice. "This mission isn't a test, Scarlet. It's survival. Over there, your training won't matter if you don't trust your instincts."

"And what about you?" she asked. "Can I trust you?"

His silence wasn't uncertainty — it was weight.

"I'll get you out," he said simply. "Even if it means I don't."

She didn't know how to respond to that. The words hung between them — too bold to be casual, too honest to be rehearsed.

They'd crossed a line in that moment. Not personal. Not yet. But something real. And in their world, real was rare. Real was dangerous.

By dusk, they were wheels-up — a private flight rerouted from Germany, with only two passengers, one encrypted tablet, and a sealed briefing envelope marked **"CLASSIFIED: EYES ONLY."**

Scarlet sat by the window, the clouds below them bathed in burnt orange. She could feel Boris next to her, a stillness to him that wasn't relaxation, but readiness. He wasn't sleeping. He wasn't distracted. He was watching. Thinking. Planning.

"Why me?" she asked finally, eyes still on the horizon.

Boris didn't answer right away. When he did, his voice was quieter than she expected.

"They chose you because you speak five languages, can read a room in seconds, and know how to become invisible in plain sight. You're not just the bait. You're the weapon."

Scarlet turned toward him. "That's not a compliment."

"It's not meant to be." He paused. "It's a warning."

She looked away, her mind circling back to Drakov. Was he already in the country? Did he know she was coming? Had he anticipated her move before she made it?

And more importantly... did he want her to come?

Her fingers brushed against the chain at her neck — the locket. She hadn't worn it for sentiment tonight. It was instinct. A reminder of her real name. Her real life. Of everything she wasn't allowed to show.

"You've worked with Viper before," she said quietly.

Boris didn't flinch. "He was different then."

"And now?"

Boris turned his head slightly, eyes distant. "Now, he's the kind of man who makes you believe things — even when you know better. That makes him the most dangerous of all."

Scarlet said nothing. Because she already knew.

They touched down under cover of night. No lights. No fanfare. Just a soft landing on an abandoned airstrip near the Belarusian border. The air outside was bitter, sharp, soaked with cold and history. Boris led the way, silent and sure-footed, moving like a man who had done this a hundred times before.

They reached the safehouse — a quiet townhouse in a forgotten part of the city. Brick façade, creaking floorboards, and curtains that hadn't been changed since the Cold War. It was perfect.

Boris handed her a burner phone and a key.

"Keep the curtains closed. Lights low. No outside calls. We move at zero six hundred."

Scarlet took the key. "And until then?"

Boris gave her a look. "Sleep. You'll need it."

She nodded, but they both knew she wouldn't sleep.

As she closed the bedroom door behind her, Scarlet leaned against the wall and let herself breathe for the first time in hours. She'd crossed borders tonight — physical, emotional, professional. And something told her there was no going back.

She was in now.

Not just in the mission.

But in something else. Something deeper.

And she couldn't tell if it started the moment she saw Boris...

...or the moment she'd walked into that garden with Victor Drakov.

Scarlet lay on the thin mattress, staring at the cracked ceiling as Boris's words echoed in her mind: *The greatest spies never fall in love. It's the one rule we never break.*

And for the first time in her career, Scarlet wasn't so sure she could keep that rule

She lay still for a long time, the silence of the safehouse louder than gunfire. Her body ached from travel, but her mind wouldn't rest. Not when her instincts were on high alert and her thoughts kept circling the two men who had suddenly upended her carefully controlled world. One — a mentor she hadn't asked for, but might have needed more than she realized. The other — a threat dressed as desire. And both, in different ways, felt too close to the pieces of herself she was supposed to keep buried.

Scarlet had always followed the rules. No attachments. No emotional interference. She was sharp because she was untethered — a shadow that passed through lives without leaving a mark. But now... something had changed. She wasn't just reading her targets anymore. She was feeling something. Reacting. And that made her vulnerable in ways that couldn't be written into a debriefing report.

Boris Volkov was a mystery she couldn't shake. In the span of one flight, he'd said less than most rookies did in a training session, and yet she felt like he'd told her more than anyone ever had. He didn't posture. He didn't lecture. He just *was* — steady, strong, experienced. A presence that didn't demand her trust, but made her want to offer it anyway. That was new. And it was terrifying.

She found herself remembering the way his voice had dropped when he warned her about instinct. The way his gaze lingered a moment longer than necessary in the conference room. The way he hadn't smiled — not once — but something in his expression had softened when she spoke. She didn't want to assign meaning to it. But she couldn't ignore it, either.

Scarlet sat up slowly, the sheet falling to her waist as she stared out the window at the frozen street below. The city outside didn't care about her dilemma. It had seen decades of betrayal and bloodshed and buried secrets. Whatever she was feeling — curiosity, confusion, or something dangerously close to longing — it wouldn't matter here. Feelings didn't keep you alive in the field. Precision did.

Still, her fingers reached instinctively for the chain around her neck. She clutched the pendant as if it could anchor her, remind her who she was. Not just the woman in the emerald dress who had played chess with Victor Drakov in a moonlit garden. Not just the agent riding shotgun next to a man whose eyes seemed to read her like a file. But Scarlet. The real Scarlet — whose father had vanished into this same maze of espionage and lies, and who had sworn never to let that darkness consume her too.

But now, standing at the edge of something she couldn't name, Scarlet felt the rules shifting beneath her feet. She had been trained to adapt — to bend without breaking. What no one ever warned her about was what to do when you *wanted* to cross the line. When the danger felt personal. When it started to matter.

The sound of a door creaking open jolted her upright. Soft footsteps moved down the hallway outside. Not hurried. Not secretive. Just... there. Her hand moved toward her gun on the nightstand, purely out of reflex. But then a voice — quiet, familiar — floated through the silence.

"You don't sleep much, do you?"

It was Boris.

Scarlet paused, then stepped out of the bedroom, barefoot, wrapped in a blanket, her hair falling in soft waves down her back. She found him in the kitchen, standing by the sink, pouring hot water over dark tea leaves in a chipped ceramic cup. The light above the stove cast a soft glow over his features — tired, worn, but still impossibly composed.

"Old habits," she said, voice low. "I don't like stillness. It feels... exposed."

Boris nodded, not looking at her. "Stillness is when the real thoughts show up."

She leaned against the doorway, watching him. "And what thoughts are showing up for you tonight?"

He handed her the cup and looked at her fully. His eyes, dark and unreadable, settled on hers. "The kind I'm not supposed to have." Scarlet didn't answer at first. The heat from the mug seeped into her hands, grounding her as much as his words had just unsteadied her. She'd spent years parsing coded messages and micro expressions, trained to spot deception in a heartbeat. But this wasn't a lie. It wasn't a deflection. What she saw in Boris's eyes was real. And real was harder to navigate than any mission.

Scarlet was conflicted for having feelings for two men... both spies...

She moved to the table slowly, sitting opposite him. The silence between them wasn't awkward — it was dense. Charged. The kind of silence that carried weight, because both of them knew what wasn't being said.

"I didn't think you were the kind of man who let himself have thoughts like that," she said quietly, not challenging, just curious.

Boris leaned back in the chair, the wood creaking beneath him. "I didn't used to be."

Scarlet studied him. He looked older tonight, though not tired. There was a weariness to him, but it wasn't about physical exhaustion — it was emotional, layered in experience, shaped by loss. His gaze drifted toward the window, toward the city sleeping under a cold moon. "This job... it doesn't let you keep much. Not friends. Not lovers. Sometimes not even your name. The only thing you have left is silence."

She felt that.

She lived that.

"And now?" she asked.

He glanced at her again, this time slower. "Now, I'm sitting across from someone who reminds me what it's like to want something for no strategic reason. No angle. No agenda."

Scarlet swallowed hard, heat crawling up the back of her neck. She hated that she didn't know what to say. She hated even more that a part of her didn't want him to stop talking.

"This isn't a good idea," she murmured, not quite looking at him.

"It's the worst idea," he agreed, without hesitation. "You're new. You're brilliant. You still have a chance to make it through this without being haunted by people like me."

She smiled faintly. "Too late."

Boris leaned forward slightly, resting his forearms on the table, his voice quieter now — more vulnerable than she had expected from a man like him. "I've buried partners. Betrayed people I cared about. Lied to women who trusted me. There's nothing in me that deserves to be wanted."

Scarlet met his gaze head-on. "I never said I wanted you."

There was a pause. A shift in the air between them.

"You didn't have to," he said.

And that was the moment she knew: this line they were dancing on — it wasn't just thin. It was already cracking.

Because no matter how many missions she survived, how many faces she wore, or how deeply she buried herself in duty, the truth was louder now than any silence had ever been.

She wanted him.

And that terrified her more than Drakov ever could.

Part II: Love in the Line of Fire

Chapter 4: The Safehouse & The Soldier

The night was a shroud, concealing their retreat as Scarlet gripped the steering wheel of the stolen sedan. The engine's hum was the only sound between them, except for Boris's ragged breathing. The events of the previous evening seemed like a blur, a chaotic sequence of decisions that led them here—fleeing the safehouse and driving through winding, desolate roads under the cover of darkness. The ambush had come swiftly, catching them off guard, and now they were running, with no clear destination but survival in mind.

As they drove, Scarlet couldn't help but think about how it had all unfolded. The night before, after completing their mission, they had decided to move. The agency's orders were clear: get in and out, lay low, and avoid unnecessary risk. But things had gone wrong. An unanticipated tip-off had set the plan into motion, and what should have been a quiet extraction turned into a battle for their lives. The mission had gone from routine to desperate, and now, they were paying the price.

With Boris injured and struggling to stay conscious beside her, something shifted within Scarlet. She had always prided herself on keeping her emotions in check, focusing solely on the task at hand. But the sight of Boris, vulnerable and hurt, stirred something in her she wasn't prepared to face. She had been trained for detachment, for staying distant, yet here she was, feeling the pull between duty and something far more complicated. She wasn't supposed to feel this way, not for someone who had lived a life as dangerous as his. But as she glanced at him again, her chest tightened, and for the first time, she questioned her ability to stay cold and focused.

She wasn't sure how she had let herself care about him, about the man who had always been her partner, her equal. They had never spoken of it, but the connection between them had always been there—silent, unspoken, until now. Now, it was harder to ignore the depth of her feelings. She wasn't sure what to do with them. It wasn't just the mission anymore. And as the hum of the engine filled the space between them, she realized they were no longer just fugitives, there was something deeper at play. Something that terrified her as much as the danger outside.

The ambush had come out of nowhere—clean, fast, and brutal. They'd just left the drop point when the first shot shattered the rear windshield. Scarlet swerved hard, tires screeching as more gunfire erupted from the treeline. Boris had pushed her down instinctively, returning fire through the open passenger window.

Then came the searing pain. One of the rounds clipped him low in the side—enough to wound, not enough to kill. He didn't even register it at first, adrenaline masking the damage. But by the time they'd lost their pursuers, the blood was already soaking through his shirt.

Blood seeped through his fingers, pressed tightly against his side.

"Just a little longer," Scarlet murmured, her voice a mix of determination and fear. "We're almost there."

Boris managed a weak nod, his usual stoic demeanor faltering under the weight of his injury.

The safehouse was a relic from a bygone era—a secluded cabin nestled deep within the Eastern European forest. Scarlet had memorized its location during mission briefings, but seeing it now, silhouetted against the moonlit sky, it felt more like a forgotten memory than a tangible refuge.

She parked the car a safe distance away, helping Boris out of the passenger seat. He leaned heavily on her, each step a testament to his fading strength.

Inside, the cabin was sparse but functional. Scarlet guided Boris to the worn-out couch, quickly assessing his wound. The bullet had grazed his side, but the bleeding was relentless.

"You'll be okay," she assured him, more for her own benefit than his. "I need to stop the bleeding."

Boris's hand caught hers, his grip surprisingly strong. "Scarlet," he rasped, "you need to be careful. We don't know if they followed us."

She met his gaze, seeing the concern etched in his features. "I'll secure the perimeter after I take care of you."

He nodded, relinquishing control—a rarity for a man accustomed to command.

Scarlet worked quickly, retrieving the first aid kit stashed beneath the floorboards. She cleaned the wound, her hands steady despite the turmoil within. Boris hissed in pain but remained silent, his eyes never leaving her face.

As she bandaged him, Scarlet couldn't help but notice the scars that marred his torso—each one a story, a testament to battles fought and survived.

"You've been through a lot," she whispered, more to herself than to him.

Boris's lips curved into a faint smile. "Comes with the territory."

She finished her work, sitting back on her heels. "That should hold for now. But you need rest."

Boris closed his eyes, exhaustion overtaking him. Scarlet watched him for a moment before standing, her own fatigue threatening to consume her. But there was no time for rest. She needed to ensure their safety.

Securing the cabin was second nature—checking locks, setting up rudimentary alarms, and familiarizing herself with potential escape routes. Satisfied, she returned to Boris's side, finding him asleep but restless.

She settled into a chair nearby, the weight of the day's events pressing down on her. The line between duty and emotion blurred as she watched over him, the walls she'd meticulously built around her heart beginning to crumble.

The morning light filtered through the cabin's grimy windows, casting a soft glow on Boris's face. He stirred, eyes fluttering open to find Scarlet watching him.

"Morning," she greeted softly, a hint of relief in her tone.

Boris attempted to sit up, grimacing as pain lanced through his side.

"Easy," Scarlet admonished, moving to assist him. "You're not invincible."

He chuckled, a sound that warmed the cold cabin. "Don't let the others hear you say that."

She smiled, the tension between them easing. "How are you feeling?"

"Like I got shot," he replied wryly. "But I'll survive."

A comfortable silence settled over them, the unspoken bond between them growing stronger.

Scarlet hesitated before speaking. "Boris, last night... I saw your scars."

His expression darkened slightly, but he nodded for her to continue.

"Each one tells a story, doesn't it?"

He sighed, running a hand through his disheveled hair. "Yes. Some stories are better left untold."

She reached out, her fingers grazing his hand. "Sometimes sharing them helps."

Boris studied her, the walls he'd built around his past wavering. "I was young when I joined the military. Eager, idealistic. I believed in the cause, in protecting my country."

Scarlet listened intently, sensing the weight of his words.

"But war changes you," he continued. "You see things, do things, that haunt you. The scars... they're reminders of the price we pay."

She squeezed his hand gently. "You're not alone in that."

Boris looked at her, truly seeing her. "And you? What ghosts do you carry?"

Scarlet took a deep breath; the memories she'd buried surfacing. "I was recruited fresh out of university. They saw potential, someone who could blend in, gather intel without raising suspicion."

He nodded, encouraging her to continue.

"My first mission was a disaster," she admitted. "I trusted the wrong person. It cost lives."

Boris's grip tightened on hers. "We all have regrets, Scarlet. It's how we carry them that defines us."

She met his gaze, vulnerability shining in her eyes. "I just... I don't want to lose myself in this life."

He cupped her cheek, his thumb brushing away a stray tear. "Then hold on to who you are. Don't let the darkness consume you."

The air between them grew charged, the line between professional and personal blurring further. But before either could act on the tension, a noise outside shattered the moment.

Scarlet was on her feet instantly, weapon drawn. Boris struggled to stand, but she pushed him back down.

"Stay here," she ordered. "I'll check it out."

He opened his mouth to protest but saw the determination in her eyes and relented.

Scarlet moved silently, every sense on high alert. She peered through the window, spotting a figure approaching the cabin cautiously.

Heart pounding, she positioned herself by the door, ready to confront the intruder.

The door creaked open slowly, and Scarlet pressed her gun against the figure's temple.

"Don't move," she commanded.

The intruder froze, hands raised in surrender. "Scarlet, it's me."

Recognition dawned, and she lowered her weapon. "Sloan? What the hell are you doing here?"

Sloan stepped into the cabin, his dark figure emerging from the shadows. He was a man Scarlet knew well but rarely trusted. Agent Sloan was a senior intelligence officer in the agency, a man whose sharp mind and cold professionalism had earned him a reputation within the circles they moved in. He was the kind of man who knew how to manipulate information, play both sides, and walk away with his hands clean. He had been a part of several successful missions, and yet, there was always something off about him, something Scarlet couldn't quite pinpoint. They had worked together on a few high-stakes operations, but his loyalty had always been... questionable.

"I could ask you the same," Sloan replied, his voice calm, too calm for the situation. His eyes flicked to Boris, assessing his condition before focusing back on Scarlet. "We need to talk."

Scarlet didn't lower her guard, her eyes narrowing as she scanned him for any sign of deception. Sloan had always operated in the shadows, and his presence now made her uneasy. He was the kind of man who played the game with a level of detachment that bordered on dangerous, and at this moment, with Boris injured and the mission spiraling out of control, she wasn't sure where his true allegiance lay.

Agent Sloan stepped into the cabin, glancing at Boris. "I could ask you the same. We need to talk."

Boris struggled to his feet, wincing. "About?"

Sloan's expression was grim. "Drakov. He's made his move."

Scarlet exchanged a glance with Boris, the weight of their reality crashing back down.

"Then we need to move," Boris said, determination overriding his pain.

Scarlet nodded, the brief respite they'd found in the cabin dissolving as duty called them back into the fray.

The cabin felt different now. What had briefly been a sanctuary — a fragile pocket of silence and unspoken feelings — was suddenly suffocating, closing in on them with the weight of reality. Scarlet glanced once more at Boris, his frame braced against the arm of the couch, blood drying at the corner of his shirt. The pain was still there, etched into his face, but the fire in his eyes had returned. The soldier was back, even if the man behind him hadn't fully healed.

Sloan's voice cut through the tension like a blade. "Drakov's not just gathering intel anymore. He's weaponizing it. There's chatter about an arms deal, but it's bigger than that. He's trying to dismantle the intelligence network in the East. Bit by bit."

Scarlet's jaw tightened. "What's the source?"

"Intercepted comms from the Belarusian black channel," Sloan replied, handing her a flash drive. "Encrypted, but it confirms movement. Weapons-grade material. Nuclear-adjacent tech. We think he's brokering through a proxy in the north."

Boris leaned forward, wincing but alert. "That's suicide. No one moves through that region unless they want to be ghosts."

"Which is why he's doing it," Scarlet murmured. "No footprints. No fingerprints."

The room fell quiet as the implications sank in. Drakov wasn't playing a game anymore — he was escalating. And they were already two steps behind.

Boris stood slowly, his movements stiff but deliberate. "We need to move before he disappears again. Once he's over the border, we lose him for good."

Scarlet looked at him. "You're still healing."

He didn't flinch. "I'll heal on the way."

The corner of her mouth twitched. *Stubborn bastard.*

But something in her chest tightened. A part of her wanted to tell him to stay — just for one more day. One more hour. That maybe, for once, someone else could do the chasing, the fighting, the risking. But that wasn't who Boris was. And it wasn't who she was, either. This life didn't make room for caution. It demanded sacrifice.

Sloan cleared his throat. "There's a contact waiting just outside the valley. Former informant. Local. Sketchy as hell, but loyal to our side — at least for now. He can get you close without alerting the wrong people."

Scarlet nodded, already calculating the next step, the next move, the next mask to wear.

As Sloan left to prep their exit route, she turned back to Boris. He was steadying himself against the wall now, testing his balance. She stepped forward, close enough to smell the sharp edge of antiseptic and the faint trace of smoke still clinging to his shirt.

"You don't have to prove anything," she said quietly.

Boris's eyes met hers. Tired. Resolved. "I'm not. I just don't know how to be anything but this."

Scarlet felt her breath hitch — not from what he said, but the truth behind it. The quiet resignation of a man who'd given so much of himself to a cause that never gave back. And suddenly, she didn't see the operative or the war-hardened soldier — she saw the fracture lines running just beneath the surface.

"We'll finish this," she said, softer now. "Together."

His expression shifted just slightly — a flicker of something warmer, something more personal than orders or mission plans.

"We better," he said, "because I'm not letting you out there without me."

Scarlet turned away quickly, hiding the heat that threatened to rise to her cheeks. The moment was over. But it had happened. And it left a mark.

Not a scar. Not yet. But maybe something deeper.

And in their line of work, those were the hardest wounds to survive.

The wind had picked up outside, rattling the loose shutters on the cabin windows. Scarlet stood by the door, watching the trees shift in the distance. Shadows danced through the forest — flickers of movement that might've been wind or might've been more. But for now, they were alone. For now, they had time.

Behind her, Boris moved quietly, retrieving the last of the supplies from a hidden panel in the floorboards. His movements were slower than usual — stiff, deliberate — but there was no mistaking the purpose in them. Pain meant nothing when you'd trained yourself to ignore it. He didn't complain. He didn't need to.

Scarlet didn't offer help. Not out of coldness, but because she understood. Sometimes, dignity was the last thing a person had left to hold onto.

The silence between them stretched — but it wasn't empty. It was full. Full of things neither of them dared say. Gratitude. Admiration. Fear. That strange, undefined current that had started back in that conference room and only grown stronger with every hour spent together. It sat in the room with them like a third presence — not entirely welcome, but impossible to ignore.

"I used to think the mission was the only thing that mattered," Scarlet said suddenly, not turning around. "That if I could just keep the lines clear — feelings out, facts in — then I'd never lose control."

Boris didn't answer, but she felt his gaze on her, steady and patient.

"But lately…" She hesitated, then exhaled. "Lately I'm realizing that control doesn't always mean strength. Sometimes it's just another kind of fear."

She turned to face him. He was standing still now, his expression unreadable — but not unfeeling.

"We walk into fire," she said. "We lie, we seduce, we kill. But the hardest thing? Is being seen."

Boris stepped closer, slowly, like he was crossing some invisible line.

"I see you," he said.

The words hit harder than a bullet.

Scarlet blinked, once. Twice. Then nodded, not trusting her voice.

Outside, the forest rustled like it was holding its breath. The world was shifting again — back into danger, back into mission mode. But something had changed in the cabin. Not loud. Not dramatic. Just real.

And in their world, real was rarer than safe houses, clean exits, or clean hands.

Scarlet moved toward the door, tightening the strap on her bag. "Let's go," she said. "Before the world finds us again."

Boris followed her, limping but upright, the weight of the next chapter already heavy on their shoulders.

They stepped into the night together — two shadows bound not just by duty anymore, but by something far harder to name.

And as the cabin disappeared behind them, so did the illusion that this mission would ever be just another operation.

It was already personal.

Chapter 5: The Betrayal

The safehouse was already gone by the time they reached the rendezvous point. What was supposed to be a quiet extraction — a clean, silent handoff of critical data — had turned into a trap. The kind that didn't leave survivors.

Scarlet crouched behind a rusted-out truck in the abandoned rail yard, her breath catching in short, controlled bursts. Gunfire echoed off the crumbling buildings, tracer rounds lighting up the dark like shooting stars made of rage and metal.

"Three o'clock!" Boris barked, dragging her down just as a bullet tore through the side mirror above her head. Shards of glass rained down, slicing her cheek.

Scarlet didn't flinch. She rolled onto her stomach and returned fire with precision, catching one of the assailants in the thigh. He went down hard, screaming in Russian.

"We were burned," she said flatly, her voice like flint striking steel.

Boris didn't respond immediately. He was already scanning the upper windows, anticipating the next wave of gunmen. But she saw the flicker in his eyes — not surprise. Not fear. **Recognition**.

"Someone from the inside," he said. "They knew the route, the timing… all of it."

Scarlet's mind raced. The plan had been airtight. Satellite drops, encrypted flash drive embedded in the cement wall of a defunct train tunnel, exfil in thirty minutes or less. The only ones who knew were the two of them, Sloan… and HQ.

And someone at HQ wanted them dead.

They managed to escape only because Boris had insisted, they take the longer, less direct route out — another of his gut calls that had saved their lives more than once. But even that hadn't been enough to avoid the ambush entirely.

A full tactical team had been waiting. Not amateurs. Not Drakov's mercs. These were trained elite Russian black ops operatives — highly trained, state-sponsored, and unmistakably brutal. The ambush had Moscow's fingerprints all over it, but the timing… the route… it still felt like someone on the inside had tipped them off."

Scarlet ducked into a storage container; Boris close behind her. She slammed the rusted door shut and bolted it from the inside, heart pounding in her ears.

"How deep does it go?" she asked, whispering.

Boris was already pulling a spare comm unit from his pack. "Deep enough that we can't trust anyone. Not even Sloan. Not anymore."

Scarlet's stomach turned. She thought back to the cabin, to the flash drive, to Sloan's quiet urgency. Had he known? Or had he just been the messenger, unaware he was setting them up?

It didn't matter now. They were cut off.

No extraction team. No safehouse. No comms link to Langley.

Just them — and a trail of corpses left in their wake.

By morning, the bodies had gone cold, and Scarlet and Boris had disappeared.

They traveled in silence, ditching their vehicle on a back road in rural Poland and continuing on foot. A truck stop gave them a temporary reprieve — new clothes, burner phones, and the knowledge that their names were already being flagged in the system.

"Scarlet checked the dark-net chatter on the burner phone they'd picked up. Their names were on an internal leak board — flagged not only as fugitives but as suspected double agents. The agency had framed them for the very data theft they'd been sent to intercept. Someone inside had spun the narrative fast. The mission dossier had been scrubbed, their comms access revoked, and their tracker beacons reassigned to decoy locations. In the official logs, they had turned. And that made them expendable."

They were now classified as "rogue." Their faces were circulating through every digital surveillance network in Europe.

They were no longer assets. They were liabilities. Ghosts the agency would erase before questions could be asked.

Scarlet looked over at Boris, who was nursing a cracked rib and a bruised shoulder beneath his fresh jacket. His eyes were different now. Not colder — just sharper. Focused. Like the betrayal hadn't wounded him… just reminded him that this was how the world worked.

"Where do we go?" she asked as they sat in the back of a supply van they'd stolen from a distribution yard.

Boris looked out at the horizon. "Off the grid. Eastern Alps. There's an old network cell I ran with, years ago. They'll help. Or they'll kill us. Either way, we'll get answers."

Scarlet almost smiled. "Comforting."

But she felt it too — the tightening in her chest, not from fear, but clarity. She had always known this job could end with a bullet, a betrayal, or a fall from grace. But she hadn't expected to be hunted by the very people she'd bled for.

They made it to a small town near the Austrian border by nightfall, ducking into an abandoned chapel on the outskirts. Boris had pulled out a weathered metal box hidden beneath a loose floorboard — part of an old dead-drop he'd established during a Cold War-era op.

Inside were documents. Weapons. Currency. And a list of names — people he once trusted.

"We have one shot," he said as Scarlet leafed through the papers. "Someone on this list has the answer. One of them either set us up… or they know who did."

Scarlet's fingers paused over a name. Agent Lera Antonov.

"She was my handler, briefly," Boris said quietly. "We had a falling out."

Scarlet raised a brow. "Falling out or fallout?"

Boris didn't answer.

The tension between them had grown since the ambush — not because of distrust, but because the stakes had changed. It was no longer just about Drakov or the data. It was about survival. It was about revenge. And beneath that — buried, but beating — was something even more dangerous.

Connection.

She knew what it was now. What she'd been ignoring. That quiet pull every time Boris looked at her like she was more than just another agent.

But now wasn't the time.

Now, they needed to disappear — and find the rat in their own house.

That night, sleep was out of the question.

Scarlet stood at the edge of the chapel window, moonlight cutting across the floor, dust shimmering in its beam like falling ash. Behind her, Boris sat with his back against the wall, reassembling a silencer in the dark.

"They'll send someone else," she said without turning around. "To finish what the ambush didn't."

"They'll send their best," Boris replied.

Scarlet turned to him. "Then we better become worse."

He glanced up at her then, and for a moment, something passed between them — a silent agreement. A new line crossed. They weren't just agents anymore. They were *allies*. Partners. Fugitives bound by survival and truth.

And maybe something else.

"We go to Zurich," Boris said. "Antonov is embedded in the UN's intelligence liaison office. If anyone knows who's pulling the strings, it's her."

Scarlet nodded. "Then we go dark. No phones. No digital trail."

Boris gave her a look. "You're learning."

"I've had a hell of a teacher."

And with that, the two vanished again — no country, no home, no orders. Just a mission:

"Find the traitor. Expose the real mole. Clear their names — not just to save themselves, but to stop an agency-wide collapse that could follow. The intel they were blamed for leaking had already started spreading. Nuclear codes. Deep-cover operatives. The kind of information that could dismantle everything they'd worked to protect. Clearing their names wasn't just personal — it was about preventing the next global catastrophe."

But Scarlet knew deep down — once the agency turned on you, there was no going back.

And she wasn't sure she wanted to.

Because in that moment — in that forgotten chapel with a silencer on the floor and the scent of dust clinging to their skin — Scarlet realized something she hadn't dared to admit until now: the version of herself that had once believed in rules and orders and the black-and-white definition of loyalty... that version was dead. Killed not by a bullet or betrayal, but by disillusionment.

What remained was sharper. Wilder. Still her — but stripped of the polish. The agency's golden girl had been reduced to the woman staring out that window, hunted, hardened, and quietly unafraid. And the terrifying part? That woman didn't miss the old Scarlet at all.

Boris watched her as if he could see the shift happen. Not with judgment, but with recognition. Maybe because he'd gone through his own version of that transformation long ago. He had always operated in gray — morally flexible, emotionally armored, quietly dangerous. But Scarlet? She was still becoming. Still burning through old beliefs to uncover something rawer underneath.

"We'll need a new alias for you," Boris said, finally breaking the silence.

She blinked, turning to him. Sophia Blake is burned. Viper exposed everything at the garden party. That cover's dead now — and so is Scarlet if we're not careful.

He nodded. "Too many eyes on that name now. If you're staying in this — really staying — you'll need to be someone else for a while."

Scarlet gave a small, sardonic smile. "I'm already someone else."

He stood, slowly, favoring his injured side. "That's not what I meant."

They held each other's gaze for a beat too long. Not professionally. Not even platonically. It wasn't romantic yet either —

not fully — but it sat on the edge of something combustible. The kind of connection forged not in candlelight and wine, but in blood, silence, and the echo of shared trauma.

Boris finally looked away and opened the rusted storage chest beside him. Inside were three passports, each more elaborate in their forgery than the last. He handed her one.

"Elena Kessler," he said. "Swiss diplomatic clearance. Gets us into Zurich without setting off alarms."

Scarlet flipped open the passport, staring at the face that was hers and yet wasn't. The name tasted foreign on her tongue. Elena. Diplomat. The irony was sharp enough to draw blood.

She closed the passport slowly, the edges rough against her fingertips. "And who will you be?"

Boris smirked faintly. "Someone who gets shot a lot, apparently."

A soft chuckle escaped her lips — the first real laugh in days. It surprised her, how easy it was to let her guard down in his presence. Not because he made her feel safe, but because he never pretended she needed saving.

She tucked the forged passport into her coat pocket and stepped away from the window, her silhouette briefly swallowed by the dim light spilling from a broken overhead lamp. Dust motes floated around her like ghosts. There was something sacred about that chapel — not because of its religion, but because of what it represented. A crossroads. A moment suspended between who she had been, and who she was about to become.

Scarlet didn't speak as she packed up what few things they'd take with them. Her movements were clean, practiced. She moved like a woman with purpose — a woman who had stopped looking for someone to follow and instead decided to lead herself through the fire.

Boris said nothing either. He watched her quietly, recognizing the transformation. The agency had recruited her for her adaptability, her precision. But this was different. This wasn't about orders. This was personal now. And that made her dangerous.

When they stepped outside, the cold bit hard. A steel-gray dawn was crawling across the horizon, casting long shadows through the overgrown cemetery surrounding the chapel. No sounds but the crunch of gravel beneath their boots and the wind whispering through headstones. The kind of silence only fugitives appreciated.

Scarlet paused at the edge of the property, glancing back one last time at the chapel. Not out of sentiment, but out of habit. Never leave a place without remembering the exits. It was the first lesson she'd ever learned in fieldwork. It applied to buildings. To missions. And maybe even to people.

"This will get worse before it gets better," Boris said beside her, his breath misting the air.

"It already has," she replied.

But there was no fear in her voice — only steel. She was no longer the operative waiting for approval. She was the one writing the rules now. And if that meant going dark, staying two steps ahead of the agency that had trained her, and burning every bridge along the way, then so be it.

They walked away from the chapel as the sky lightened. Two ghosts. Two weapons. Neither with a country, a handler, or a safety net.

Only each other.

And in this world — that was either the most dangerous liability, or the last hope they had.

Chapter 6: The First Kiss

They'd crossed two borders under forged identities, using the UN diplomat alias Scarlet had picked up from Boris's contact in Zurich. A stolen Peugeot, an unguarded mountain road, and three tense hours through Slovakia had landed them in Budapest by sunrise. It wasn't part of the original plan, but nothing was anymore. The city was neutral ground—unmonitored, fractured, unpredictable. Just the way they needed it.

The safehouse in Budapest was nothing like the one in the forest. This one was urban — slick and quiet, a top-floor apartment tucked between two brutalist towers with peeling stucco and faded communist ghosts. The windows were covered in blackout panels. The water ran slow and brown for the first few minutes. The silence was heavier here, not peaceful like the chapel had been — it was loaded.

Scarlet paced the length of the narrow hallway, her bare feet silent on the cold wooden floor.

Zurich hadn't gone according to plan. Antonov's contact had turned up dead—a clean hit, execution-style, the kind that sent a message. Worse, their presence had triggered a silent alarm buried in the security grid. Scarlet barely got them out before the building went into lockdown. Whatever Antonov was hiding, she was willing to kill for it. And now, they were back in the wind.

It was their third day off the grid since Zurich, and tension clung to the air like smoke that refused to clear. She hadn't spoken much. Neither had Boris. Not out of anger, but because words felt clumsy for what was happening between them — for what wasn't being said.

She passed the open bathroom door, catching a glimpse of herself in the cracked mirror.

The woman staring back at her wasn't the same operative who stepped into Zurich, or hid out in the chapel, or even pulled the trigger in Geneva. Every stop along this mission had carved a new edge into her—sharpening the blade she was becoming.

Her hair was damp, curling slightly around her face, her cheeks flushed from the chill and the heat beneath her skin. Her eyes had changed too. Sharper. More tired. But alive. *God, she felt alive.*

She found Boris in the kitchen, leaning over a map splayed across the table, shirtless, bruised, and backlit by the low orange glow of the single hanging bulb. His skin was mottled from the last fight — angry purple marks across his ribs, fresh bandages taped at his side. He hadn't noticed her yet. Or maybe he had, and he was pretending not to. Either way, it didn't matter.

She stopped in the doorway.

"You're bleeding again," she said softly.

"I've had worse," he replied without looking up.

"You keep saying that."

"Because it's true."

Scarlet stepped into the room, slowly, her voice quieter now. "You're not invincible, Boris."

That made him glance at her. Just once. And for a moment, the air between them thickened. His eyes moved over her face — the softness that still lingered despite the violence of their world. The pain there, too. And something else. Something he wouldn't let himself name.

"You should sleep," he said.

"So should you."

He pushed away from the table, standing upright. The tension in his body was unmistakable — not just physical, but emotional. As if being near her was some kind of silent battle he was losing by inches.

Scarlet moved first. She reached out, just enough to graze her fingers along the side of his jaw. His breath caught.

And then, he looked at her like she wasn't just a colleague. Like she wasn't just a weapon forged for the mission. He looked at her like she was the only thing in the room that mattered. His hand came up, slow, hesitant, settling gently at her waist.

They didn't speak.

They didn't have to.

Because when his mouth found hers, it wasn't sweet.

It was years of silence, every buried feeling, every near-death moment, every second of pretending they didn't care — poured into one kiss that unraveled both of them.

Scarlet kissed him like she might never get another chance. Like kissing him was the only honest thing she'd ever done. And Boris kissed her like it might destroy him, but he was already too far gone to stop it.

His hand slipped up her back, pulling her closer, the pressure of his body against hers grounding and electric at once. Her fingers curled into the edge of his waistband, just enough to make him inhale sharply.

And then — he pulled away.

Abruptly.

Painfully.

She stood there, stunned, lips parted, heart thudding loud in her chest.

Boris stepped back like the touch had burned him. His jaw clenched. His voice was low, rough, frayed.

"We can't."

Scarlet swallowed. "Why not?"

He looked at her for a long, aching moment. "Because this life doesn't allow it."

The words sliced through the heat like a blade.

She held his gaze, refusing to look away. "You don't believe that."

"I have to," he said, quieter now. "Because the second I let myself want something—someone—it becomes a liability. And I can't afford that. Not with you."

Her chest ached. Not just from rejection — but from the truth in it.

She stepped back, folding her arms over herself like armor. "Then don't kiss me like that again."

Boris nodded, slowly, as if punishing himself.

"I won't," he said.

But they both knew he was lying.

Because the way he looked at her in that moment — like she was the last true thing in a world built on false flags and disappearing names — that wasn't something a man could pretend away. Not even someone like Boris, who had spent half a lifetime swallowing his own feelings just to survive the long corridors of deception. He could tell himself a hundred times that the mission came first, that feelings made you soft, that emotions were a liability. But that kiss had broken something. Cracked it wide open. And once something like that surfaced, it didn't go back down. Not easily. Not cleanly.

Scarlet didn't push him. Not that night. Instead, she walked past him, her jaw tight, her heart still slamming against her ribs like it was trying to escape. She moved into the small bedroom at the end of the hall, closed the door quietly, and didn't look back. She sat on the edge of the cot for a long time, listening to the faint city sounds outside — the distant echo of tires on wet pavement, the low hum of Budapest at night, the rhythm of a world that had no idea two fugitives were holed up just six stories above it, wrestling with their own cold wars.

Her fingers touched her lips without thinking. They were still swollen, still warm. That kiss had stripped her bare — not physically, but emotionally. There had been nothing tactical about it, nothing calculated. It wasn't a seduction meant to open doors or compromise a target. It had been real. Raw. And it terrified her. Because if she felt something real in this life — something human — then maybe she wasn't the weapon she had trained to become. Maybe she'd already lost control of her own detachment. Maybe she wanted to.

Boris didn't sleep that night. He sat on the floor of the living room, leaning against the cold concrete wall, eyes fixed on the slats of shadow stretching across the ceiling from the half-open blinds. His gun rested beside him, untouched, while his mind circled that kiss like a soldier circling the ruins of a bombed-out building. There was no denying it. No rationalizing it away. He had kissed her like a dying man reaching for something holy. And he'd pulled back because he knew — knew in his bones — that if he let it happen again, he wouldn't be able to stop.

He'd made that mistake once before. A long time ago. Different city. Different woman. But the result had been the same — Loss. Guilt. Consequences that spiraled like smoke across every mission after. He had sworn never again. Never mix personal with professional. Never let emotions compromise the op. But then Scarlet Swanson had walked into his life with those sea-glass eyes and that infuriating mix of precision and fire, and suddenly, every promise he'd made to himself started unraveling.

The next morning, the sun broke early, bright and indifferent. Scarlet was already in the kitchenette by the time Boris emerged, dressed in gray sweats, hair still damp from the sink. She didn't look at him. She poured black coffee into two mismatched mugs and pushed one toward him on the counter without a word. The gesture was mechanical. Efficient. But the silence that wrapped around them was anything but casual.

Boris took the coffee and leaned against the counter. "We'll leave tonight," he said. His voice was flat, professional.

Scarlet nodded once. "Destination?"

"Vienna. One of Antonov's old contacts surfaced. He'll talk. But not for long. We need to be there before her people catch wind."

Scarlet didn't respond right away. She sipped her coffee, eyes fixed on the opposite wall. "Do you think he's the leak?"

Boris hesitated. "I think he knows who is."

That was the closest he'd come to hope in weeks. But he didn't allow himself to feel it fully. Hope was too fragile. Too easily broken. Like feelings. Like people.

They moved through the day with precision — checking burner phones, scanning satellite routes, analyzing traffic flow into Vienna, encrypting communication lines through a triple-veil dark web relay. The kind of grunt work that kept hands busy and minds numbed. But nothing could fully erase the electricity between them. It pulsed beneath the surface of every conversation, every glance, every small accidental touch.

By midafternoon, Scarlet sat cross-legged on the couch with a field tablet in her lap, mapping Antonov's travel patterns from the last three months. Boris hovered nearby, reading aloud from an intelligence file decrypted just hours earlier. Their coordination was flawless. Their chemistry — still visible in the way they moved around each other without words — was something no training could replicate.

But beneath it all, they were unraveling.

Because the silence between them wasn't the kind that brought peace. It was the kind that screamed.

"After Vienna," Scarlet said suddenly, not looking up, "What's your plan?"

Boris didn't answer right away. He sat down across from her, folding his hands together. "Find the traitor. Burn everything they built. Then disappear."

"And after that?"

He looked at her. "There is no after that."

Scarlet exhaled slowly. "That's the thing about people like us. We talk about revenge like it's a finish line. But what happens when it doesn't fix anything? When there's nothing left but ghosts?"

Boris met her gaze. His eyes were tired. "Then we carry them."

The weight of his words settled between them. Heavy. Inevitable. Scarlet felt the crack forming deeper inside her — that line between who she had to be and who she might have been if the world hadn't sharpened her into a blade. She didn't want to carry ghosts. Not anymore. She wanted to *feel* something again before it was all over. Even if it was reckless. Even if it got her killed.

That night, as they prepared to move, she stepped into the small bedroom again to change. The lights were dim, casting golden shadows across her shoulders. She caught her reflection in the mirror again — not for the first time — but this time she stared longer. She didn't look like the woman from Langley briefings anymore. Her face was older now. Not in years, but in miles. In choices.

When she stepped out, Boris was by the door, checking his weapon, adjusting the suppressor. He didn't look up until he felt her presence — and when he did, something shifted in his face again. Not lust. Not admiration. Just... need.

"I meant what I said," he told her quietly.

Scarlet crossed her arms. "Which part?"

"That we can't."

She nodded. "Then stop looking at me like that."

His lips parted, but he didn't speak.

"Because every time you do," she continued, "I forget that this life is supposed to be about surviving. And I start thinking about what it might feel like to *live*."

That hit him harder than a bullet.

He stepped closer. Not touching. Just enough for her to feel his breath.

"I never wanted to put you in danger," he said. "But the second I kissed you, I knew I already had."

Scarlet didn't move. "You didn't put me in danger, Boris. I walked into it the second I chose this life."

Their eyes locked.

"I'm not asking you for promises," she added. "I just need to know if I'm the only one who felt something real."

He didn't blink. "You're not."

And just like that, the distance between them became unbearable.

But they didn't touch.

Not this time.

Because some connections weren't meant to be rushed. They were meant to build — slowly, dangerously — until the whole world caught fire.

The silence after that was unbearable and sacred all at once — like standing at the edge of a cliff with no wind, no sound, just the weight of gravity reminding you that one wrong move could change everything. They stood there in the dim kitchen light, motionless, suspended in something too fragile to name and too dangerous to ignore. Scarlet didn't speak. Boris didn't retreat. But something had been decided between them, without a single word.

When Scarlet finally moved, it wasn't toward him. She stepped around him to the table, picked up her gear bag, and cinched the strap tight across her shoulder. Her heartbeat hadn't slowed, but her hands were steady. That was the part she didn't understand — how she could feel so calm when everything inside her was shifting like tectonic plates before an earthquake.

Boris joined her a beat later, slinging his own bag over one shoulder. "Car's in the garage under Unit B," he said, voice back to that mission-steeped grit. "Black Opel. Changed the plates."

She nodded. "Gassed?"

"Full tank. Cleaned the GPS. I left a trail leading toward Prague. If they're tracking us, they'll follow that first."

Scarlet allowed herself the briefest smile. "Still five steps ahead."

"It's the only way to stay alive."

But she caught the flicker in his expression. He wasn't just staying ahead to survive. He was doing it for her. And it scared the hell out of him.

As they exited the safehouse, the Budapest night wrapped around them like a dark secret. The air was crisp, kissed with the distant scent of diesel and wet stone. The city hummed quietly beneath their feet, oblivious to the storm quietly building behind the eyes of two people who had seen too much and still refused to look away from each other.

In the shadows, they moved like they always had — precise, silent, deadly. But tonight, something was different. There was a rhythm between them now, invisible but pulsing. They didn't touch. They didn't speak. But each step was a kind of promise. That no matter how dark the road ahead, they weren't walking it alone.

And maybe, in a life carved from lies, shadows, and betrayal… that was the most dangerous truth of all.

Chapter 7: The Choice

Vienna was a city made for diplomacy and deceit. Its polished streets, its historic facades, and its delicate balance between East and West had long made it a haven for spies. Everyone smiled here — diplomats in fine suits, tourists holding maps, agents in tailored shadows. And every smile hid something.

Scarlet had never felt so out of place in a city designed for masks. It wasn't the tension or the constant surveillance that unnerved her. It was the fact that for the first time, she wasn't sure which mask she was wearing.

She sat alone on a park bench in Stadtpark, the air crisp, the sky a pale gray ceiling over Vienna's ornate skyline. A small envelope rested in her gloved hands, sealed with a red wax insignia she hadn't seen in years — a backchannel from Langley. No name. No traceable courier. Just silence and implication.

She opened it slowly. Inside: a single sheet of parchment, watermarked and unambiguous.

We can offer you protection. Hand over Boris Volkov. You'll be cleared. No charges. No burn notice. You have forty-eight hours. Or you will be classified as a rogue agent. You've been warned.

Scarlet's breath caught. She read it again. Then again. But the words didn't change.

She could barely feel the cold anymore.

She walked for hours after that. Through alleys and boulevards, past cafes filled with laughter and old cathedrals heavy with silence. The city faded around her, blurring into movement and noise, but her mind was somewhere else entirely — trapped between two versions of herself.

One version believed in orders. Believed in the mission. She was sharp, clean, and righteous. She'd worked for years to build that identity. To become the agent who never blinked. Who followed through, no matter the cost.

The other version… was different.

She remembered how Boris had looked at her in Budapest. How he hadn't begged. Hadn't asked her to choose him. But had kissed her like he already knew she would.

She hated how well he knew her.

Scarlet ended up in the back of a low-lit café off Mariahilfer Strasse, drinking a bitter espresso while her thoughts spiraled. Every instinct told her to report the location. To wipe the trail clean and salvage what little of her career still remained.

But every time she imagined Boris behind a wire-glass window, interrogated, broken down, used up and discarded — she felt something deep in her ribcage snap.

Boris wasn't waiting at the safehouse when she returned. She was grateful. She wasn't ready to look him in the eye. Not yet.

Instead, she paced the apartment like a caged animal. Her fingers hovered over the burner phone twice, once to destroy it, once to call. She did neither.

She was halfway through packing when he finally stepped through the door, moving like he'd seen a ghost.

Scarlet froze.

"You're late," she said.

His face was pale. Drawn tight.

"I've been to Antonov."

That got her attention. She dropped the clothes back into the duffel and turned to face him fully.

"She gave me everything," Boris said, voice low. "Coordinates, encrypted files, old dead-drops, shadow names. Someone's been bleeding information from a covert nuclear storage program in the Baltic Sea. If the data gets out, it won't just be political leverage — it'll be war."

Scarlet felt a chill ripple through her. "Who's behind it?"

"She didn't say," he replied. "She's scared. Said the leak goes above Langley. Above Moscow. Private networks. Deep contractors. Maybe even rogue NATO cells."

"Jesus."

"She also said we weren't the only ones looking for it. Someone's moving faster than we are. And they're not playing by rules."

Scarlet's throat tightened. "Then we have to get to it first."

Boris nodded — but something in his expression was different now. Guarded.

"What?" she asked.

"You were gone a long time today."

She didn't answer.

He stepped closer. "Did they reach out to you?"

Still, she said nothing.

"Scarlet."

Her voice finally broke the silence, soft and cracked. "They offered me a way out."

That landed hard.

"And?" he asked.

She looked at him, pain blazing behind her eyes. "They want me to give you up."

Boris didn't flinch. He didn't even look surprised.

"I figured," he said.

"You're not angry?"

He stepped closer, gently, like she was a fuse about to go off. "I would've done the same if our roles were reversed."

"No," she whispered. "You wouldn't."

And that, somehow, made it worse.

The silence between them deepened. It wasn't the cold, clinical silence of operatives — it was the kind that stretched between two people standing on the edge of something irreversible.

Scarlet finally spoke. "If I turn you in, I get my life back. I'm cleared. I get to walk out of this."

"But you don't want to," Boris said quietly.

She didn't deny it.

"I don't want you to choose me because of guilt," he added. "Or loyalty. Or what happened in Budapest. I want you to choose what you can live with."

Scarlet laughed bitterly. "There is no version of this I can live with."

"You can't outrun who you are," he said.

"But I can choose who I become."

He looked at her for a long, long moment. "Then choose."

Her heart felt like it was splitting open.

And for the first time in her life — Scarlet Swanson didn't know how to save herself.

Boris didn't press her. He simply stood there, still as stone, waiting for her to catch up to the weight of her own heart. Scarlet wanted to scream at him — for being so calm, for knowing her too well, for standing there like he wasn't the most impossible choice she'd ever faced. The problem wasn't what she'd been asked to do. The problem was that part of her had considered it. Still was. And she hated that she understood exactly why.

She turned away, walking toward the window as the city lights of Vienna flickered against the fogged glass. From this height, the world looked peaceful. Civilized. Not like it was one bad decision away from detonating. "They made it sound easy," she said. "Like I could just walk away. Wash my hands of this. Forget you."

Boris's voice was quiet, almost hollow. "Could you?"

She shook her head once. "No. That's the problem."

Behind her, he moved — just a step. It was all he ever needed to shift an entire atmosphere. "Scarlet," he said, and her name in his voice broke something soft and buried.

She turned. "Tell me the truth. If it were me… if the agency gave you the same choice — would you give me up?"

He didn't blink. "No."

She studied his face, searching for the lie and finding none. It both crushed and steadied her. The kind of loyalty she'd never asked for, but couldn't ignore. "That's what makes this harder," she said. "Because I don't know if I'm that strong."

Boris took another step forward. "Strength isn't doing the thing that keeps you clean. It's doing the thing that costs you — and still standing afterward."

Scarlet looked at him, and for the first time in hours, her voice was clear. "If I choose you, I burn every bridge I've ever built."

He nodded. "Then maybe we build something better."

The words hit her like a strike to the chest — not because they were romantic, but because they were so damn real. No grand declarations. No promises of safety or happy endings. Just truth. And in their world, that was rarer than any coded intel.

She didn't move toward him. Didn't kiss him. Not yet.

But she did make a decision.

She stepped back from the window and slowly reached for the burner phone.

And smashed it to pieces against the floor.

Boris exhaled, just once, like a man who'd been holding his breath for a very long time.

Outside, sirens began to wail in the distance — faint, but growing.

Because in their world, choices always had consequences.

And Scarlet had just made hers.

The phone lay shattered on the tile, its circuitry exposed like bones. The silence that followed wasn't empty — it was filled with finality. In this line of work, decisions were rarely clean. But this one was unmistakable. There would be no pretending, no spinning it later in a field debrief. Scarlet hadn't hesitated when the time came, and Boris knew what that meant. She wasn't just walking away from her agency. She was walking toward him — toward a life neither of them had ever allowed themselves to want.

He didn't speak, not yet. He just watched her, his chest rising and falling with a strange rhythm. Relief, maybe. Regret, definitely. A man like Boris had learned long ago that getting what you wanted often came at the highest cost. And right now, the woman standing in front of him had just paid it. For him.

Scarlet turned slowly, brushing her hand over the table where the envelope had been. She picked it up again, the once-pristine sheet of paper now creased and trembling slightly in her grip. "This was never a choice," she murmured. "Not really. If it had been, I would've walked away from all of it a long time ago."

Boris stepped closer, but not to comfort her. He knew better. "They'll know by now. The burner was active. It pinged when you opened the envelope. You've got maybe thirty minutes before they move."

"Then we don't waste time."

She crossed the room and began pulling out the pre-packed gear: encrypted drives, the laptop wrapped in a microfiber sheet, a passport under the name Elena Mykov — a Romanian art historian traveling to Warsaw. Scarlet had aliases like other women had shoes, but none of them had ever mattered before. Now, every step they took meant something. Every identity was a gamble.

"Vienna's not safe anymore," Boris said. "We need to go dark — full digital blackout. That means no GPS, no local comms. And no repeat routes."

She nodded, already halfway through stripping the laptop down for off-grid use. "We'll head toward Brno on foot. There's an old border trail along the riverbank. Unwatched. Once we cross, we ditch the car and disappear."

"You've done this before?"

Scarlet gave him a glance — not smug, not coy. Just honest. "I've done worse."

That earned the barest trace of a smile from Boris, but it didn't reach his eyes. They were already shifting into operational mode — something automatic, instinctual, but different this time. Because now they weren't working for orders. They were working for survival. For each other.

Scarlet strapped the backup weapon to her hip, then tucked the encrypted hard drive into the lining of her coat. "What did Antonov give you exactly?" she asked, tightening the zipper.

Boris pulled a flash drive from his inner jacket pocket, no larger than a paperclip. "Names. Transfer logs. A location in Poland. It's all tied to a cache — old Soviet stockpile buried under a tech firm that went bankrupt last year. She said the final phase is already in motion."

"And who's moving it?"

"That's the part she wouldn't say."

Scarlet's brow furrowed. "Wouldn't? Or couldn't?"

"She looked scared, Scarlet. Real fear. I don't think she's the one pulling the strings anymore. I think someone got to her."

She didn't like that. Not at all. "Then we're late."

"Not if we run now."

They both moved quickly after that. The safehouse had served its purpose, but staying another hour was suicide. Already, Scarlet's mind was mapping every escape corridor, every blind alley, every checkpoint in a five-mile radius. She wasn't just a ghost anymore — she was a threat. And she'd just declared war on the people who made her.

They exited through the freight stairs, not the main door. The building was old enough that its steel bones groaned when you touched them, but it had kept them safe — until now. Outside, Vienna's early evening haze had set in. It painted the cobbled alleys in long golden streaks that made the air feel both beautiful and ominous. The kind of beauty that only meant something if you were alive to see it tomorrow.

As they moved, Scarlet couldn't help but feel the ghost of the agency trailing her steps. She knew the tactics. She knew how they would track her. She also knew how to stay one step ahead — because they'd taught her.

"You okay?" Boris asked as they slipped through a side street near Stephansplatz.

She didn't look at him. "Ask me when this is over."

He nodded, respecting her distance, but he still walked beside her. Close enough to protect. Far enough not to be a weakness. It was a balance they'd mastered long before either of them admitted there was anything to protect at all.

A siren whined in the distance. Not close. Not yet. But it was coming. And not for a city emergency. It was for them.

By the time they reached the garage, Scarlet was already rewiring the car's navigation and swapping plates again. It took less than two minutes. She was surgical when she worked. And Boris knew better than to interrupt her now.

Once they hit the road, she took the wheel — she always did when it was time to disappear. Boris checked the rearview mirror out of habit. So far, nothing. But they both knew better. This wasn't about outrunning Langley. It was about outrunning whoever Langley was now taking orders from.

In the quiet hum of the engine, Scarlet spoke — her voice low, threaded with clarity. "When we reach Brno, we'll split. You take the intel. I'll lay down false trails."

Boris turned toward her, something tightening in his jaw. "No."

She didn't blink. "It's the smart move."

"It's the suicidal one."

"You're more valuable than I am right now."

He shook his head. "Don't ever say that again."

And just like that, the space between them wasn't professional anymore. It wasn't tactical.

It was personal. Real. Dangerous.

And it was only just beginning.

By the time they reached the Czech border, the sun had dipped behind the hills, leaving only a fading orange stain across the clouds. Scarlet drove without headlights, navigating by instinct and memory, her knuckles white around the steering wheel. In the passenger seat, Boris kept his eyes on the tree line, his silence not from fear, but focus. There was no conversation now — only the understanding that something fundamental had shifted. She had chosen. And that meant everything had changed.

They parked the car under a viaduct near the edge of Brno, a forgotten place off the grid, where wild grass grew taller than the road signs and silence stretched in every direction. Scarlet killed the engine and didn't move. The stillness of the moment wrapped around them like gauze — thin, temporary, barely holding them together. She knew this would be the last safe place for a long while. There would be no safehouses. No handlers. No backup. Just them, against a machine they'd once served.

"You sure about this?" Boris asked, voice gravel and smoke. Not doubt — just confirmation. He needed to hear it from her one more time.

Scarlet turned to him, her expression unreadable. "I wasn't made for loyalty without a conscience. They trained me to obey. You taught me to question. And I'd rather be hunted for that than honored for silence."

Boris didn't respond — not with words. He reached across the console, wrapped her hand in his, and gave a single, firm squeeze. Not affection. Not comfort. Something more primal. A pact. When their eyes met again, there were no illusions left between them. Only the brutal honesty of two people who had nothing left to hide — and no one left to trust but each other.

Above them, the night crept in, thick and black. And as they walked into the shadows side by side, neither Scarlet nor Boris looked back. The game had changed. The rules were gone. The war had found them — and they were no longer playing by anyone's code but their own.

Part III: The Final Mission

The Spy Who Loved Me: A Scarlet Swanson Story
By: Diane Wyatt

Chapter 8: The Spy Who Loved Me

After narrowly escaping their last encounter in the Czech Republic, Scarlet and Boris had made their way through the night, crossing the border into Poland in a stolen vehicle. The route had been long and cautious, avoiding major highways and sticking to remote roads that led them through the dense forests of Eastern Europe. Now, in the quiet of Warsaw, they were far from the chaos that had driven them here — but the mission was far from over.

The snow came late in the season, brushing the rooftops of Warsaw in a hush of white and blue, like the city was trying to make peace with itself. But there was no peace here — not for Scarlet, not for Boris, and certainly not for the agency that had trained them both to forget what peace felt like. They moved through the city like whispers, past frozen fountains and quiet intersections where diplomatic embassies loomed like castles, cold and impenetrable. Somewhere beneath this old skin of Europe, the final thread of betrayal pulsed — and Scarlet was going to follow it, no matter how deep it led.

They'd been in hiding for four days, tucked into the shadow of a burnt-out opera house just off the Vistula River. No signal. No paper trail. Scarlet had changed her hair, Boris had shaved his beard, and both of them moved like ghosts. Still, they weren't hiding anymore. Not really. They were preparing. The leak wasn't a myth. It wasn't some cleverly staged distraction by a foreign power. It was real — and it had teeth. If they didn't find it first, the world wouldn't just be unstable. It would burn.

The mission had changed, and so had she.

Scarlet stood at the edge of the crumbling stage, her gloved hands wrapped around a silenced SIG Sauer, scanning a digital map Boris had modified with active surveillance patches. Every blink of red meant a new surveillance hit — a drone, a human tail, or an active feed bouncing off a satellite that shouldn't have been online. "They're tracking government-grade heat signatures," Boris murmured behind her, his breath warm on her neck. "Whoever's doing this, they're not freelance."

"Langley?" she asked, though she already knew the answer.

He shook his head. "Langley would've used drones. This is internal. Someone who knows the old backchannels."

Someone like them.

They'd both expected to find dirt on the usual suspects — double agents, mole networks, black ops splinter cells. But what they'd uncovered went deeper. The leak wasn't about information. It was about leverage. Control. Someone inside the agency was feeding nuclear movement coordinates to private contractors — with the intent to trigger a global flashpoint and profit from the chaos. A manufactured war. And the man they wanted to frame for it?

Boris Volkov.

They had files to prove it now — timestamped handoffs, falsified intercepts, doctored comms logs. All pointing back to Boris. All lined up perfectly for when Scarlet was supposed to deliver him to Langley. Except she hadn't. She'd broken ranks. She'd burned her only bridge. And now, she was the one standing in front of him, blocking the shot.

Scarlet sat at the broken vanity table near the curtain wings, her fingers gliding over the folder they'd stolen from the agency's Warsaw liaison safehouse — a move that had nearly gotten them both killed. She could still feel the adrenaline pulsing beneath her skin, like a second heartbeat. The folder was thick, stamped with clearance codes she once believed were sacred. Inside it, the truth stared back at her with surgical precision: a target sheet listing Boris's name under a "containment and elimination" protocol. Not capture. Not arrest. Elimination. It was never about turning him in. They wanted him silenced.

She turned the final page and froze. There, clipped to a surveillance brief, was a photo of herself — taken only days ago. She was walking through a tram station in Prague, scarf pulled low, sunglasses angled across her cheekbones. It wasn't the photo that scared her. It was the notation: "Asset compromised. High probability of emotional conflict. Monitor and re-assess loyalty." That wasn't a threat. That was a warning — that her feelings had been flagged. That someone inside had already guessed the truth. And if they knew she'd fallen for Boris… they'd come for her too.

Behind her, Boris leaned against the far wall, reloading his weapon with methodical ease. She watched him in the mirror's broken reflection, seeing not just the man she'd run with, but the man she'd risked everything for. In another life, he would've been a soldier, a teacher, someone who came home at the end of the day. But in this world, he was a man built to be hunted — and she was the fool who loved him anyway.

"You're thinking too loud," Boris said without turning around.

Scarlet closed the folder and stood. "They flagged me."

He looked up. "For what?"

"For you."

His jaw tightened, but there was no shock in his eyes — just resignation. "Then there's no going back."

"There never was."

They moved quickly after that, slipping through side alleys and half-buried tunnels that ran beneath the city like veins. They'd memorized the layout during the Cold War reenactment drills, back when war was a game of strategy, not survival. Now, every step was measured. Every breath drawn in silence. Their destination: an old intelligence substation that had been decommissioned after the Berlin

Wall fell. Unmarked, unlit, and off every modern map. Inside, a single server remained active — the last untouched node in a secure network. And if they reached it, they could trace the intel leak back to its source.

But it wasn't just the mission pressing on Scarlet's chest as she moved. It was the memory of his hand in hers the night before, when they'd slipped into sleep side-by-side under the collapsed rafters of the opera house. They hadn't touched. They hadn't needed to. The warmth of his body near hers had been enough to quiet the storm — until morning reminded them what waited beyond the walls.

As they crossed the edge of the Vistula, Boris stopped, his hand going to her wrist. "After this… there's no hiding what we are."

Scarlet met his eyes. "I'm done hiding."

He nodded once, then pulled her behind a rusted rail barrier as two unmarked vehicles sped past — the kind used by internal security, the kind that didn't stop unless they had a target. Their timeline had shrunk. They had hours at best.

At the substation, Scarlet hacked through the old biometric lock with trembling hands, not from nerves, but because she knew what came next. Inside, the air was stale, humming with the quiet electrical pulse of a building that had been forgotten. They found the old interface console tucked behind a steel firewall, blinking like a heartbeat. Boris inserted the drive Antonov had given him. The room dimmed. The screen flickered.

Scarlet read the name aloud, her voice catching in her throat. "Mason Grey."

Boris turned. "Who?"

She handed him the dossier that had just loaded — a full agent file with photos, transfers, wire logs, and secure chat captures. "Grey. Level six asset. Operates through procurement and cyber-ops. Assigned to Brussels. But look…" She tapped the screen. "He was listed as dead. KIA. But he's been moving intel through a ghost relay in Eastern Europe. He's the leak."

"And Langley's covering it up."

Scarlet nodded. "Or using him. Which means the agency's compromised all the way up the chain."

Boris backed away from the screen. "So, what now? We dump the intel and go dark? Upload it?"

Scarlet stepped forward, her voice steel. "No. We send it somewhere it can't be buried. Press. Interpol. Hell, the UN if we have to. No redactions. Full disclosure. Let the world see what they've turned us into."

He was quiet for a beat, then: "You'll never be safe."

"I'm already not."

The upload began — a slow crawl across a fractured connection, each percent dragging like a heartbeat in a storm. And with every second, the walls closed in. Outside, a low rumble began — engines. Boots. Voices on comms.

Scarlet moved to the door. "Go. Now."

Boris stepped up behind her. "Not without you."

"You're the story. I'm just the footnote."

He grabbed her arm, spun her toward him. "No. Don't you dare say that. You're the only reason I'm still alive."

They stood there, nose to nose, the air between them charged with everything that had gone unsaid. Then, finally — like a tide that couldn't be held back — she pulled him into a kiss. It wasn't gentle. It wasn't poetic. It was a collision — desperate, wild, and full of fire. His hands cupped her face. Hers curled into his jacket. The world beyond them burned — and for once, they didn't care.

When they broke apart, it was with breathless defiance.

"You were never just the spy," he whispered. "You were the one who loved me."

"And I still do," she said, voice ragged. "But now we have to run."

Together, they grabbed the drive, erased their trail, and vanished into the tunnels just as the door burst open behind them. Gunfire echoed through the halls — but they were already gone.

And somewhere beneath the fractured sky of a world tilting toward war, the truth was out.

And so were they.

They didn't stop running until the city was miles behind them and the frost had begun to cling to their lashes. Somewhere in the foothills north of Warsaw, they found temporary shelter in an abandoned farmhouse, half-collapsed and left to rot. The windows were shattered, the roof partially caved in, but it was dry and dark, and that was all they needed. Boris locked the door behind them, checked the sightlines through the slats in the wall, then finally let himself exhale. Scarlet dropped to the wooden floor, legs trembling not from fear but from the adrenaline crash. She hadn't realized how close they'd been to dying until they were safe again. Or as safe as they could ever be.

The drive was still warm in her coat pocket, as if it carried the weight of what they'd just done. They hadn't just defied orders or exposed a traitor. They'd ripped the mask off an entire system. Somewhere, alarms were going off. Politicians were being briefed. Narratives were already being rewritten. But for the first time, Scarlet didn't care how they spun it. The truth was out. The war machine would have to look itself in the mirror. And even if they were hunted for the rest of their lives, even if they never had peace again, that would have to be enough.

They sat in silence for a long time. No plans. No strategies. Just the sound of wind howling through cracked walls and the shared knowledge that there was no turning back. Scarlet leaned her head against the wall, her breath finally steadying. "We should've died back there."

"But we didn't," Boris said, his voice low, the gravel in it softer than usual. "We made it out. Together."

That word — together — hit harder than any gunshot. It was a promise neither of them had dared make out loud, and yet here they were. Not because of orders or survival instinct. Because they chose to be. Because they'd kept choosing each other, even when it made no tactical sense. That, Scarlet realized, was the most dangerous rebellion of all.

She looked over at him, studied the man who had once been her assignment, her enemy, her partner. Now, he was something else entirely. "You know what scares me the most?" she said.

Boris met her gaze. "What?"

"That I don't regret any of it."

His smile was faint, but it held years of pain, of hope, of things he never let himself want. "Then maybe we didn't lose after all."

The quiet stretched again, but it felt different this time. Less hollow. More like a held breath. Scarlet moved closer, resting her hand against his. Not as an operative. Not as a protector. But as the woman who had given everything up — her name, her clearance, her entire damn identity — for a man she was never supposed to fall in love with. And who had, despite everything, never let her fall alone.

Outside, the world still turned. Governments scrambled to reframe what had just been unleashed. Shadow operatives began hunting for the ghosts who'd lit the fuse. But in that moment, inside a broken farmhouse in the middle of nowhere, none of that mattered. They were alive. They had each other. And that was something the agency couldn't erase, no matter how many files they burned.

Scarlet lay back against the cold wood, eyes drifting upward toward the shattered ceiling. The stars were visible through the hole — brilliant, endless, uncaring. She wondered how many times she'd stared at them on missions, searching for answers, believing she was just a small part of something larger. But maybe that was the point. Maybe the small things — the choices, the love, the people you'd give everything for — were what mattered most.

She turned toward Boris. "We don't get a happy ending."

"No," he said. "But maybe we get something real."

And this time, when they kissed, it wasn't about passion or survival or saying goodbye.

It was about finally being seen. And choosing to stay anyway.

The quiet that followed wasn't empty. It was filled with the weight of everything they didn't have to say anymore. Their walls had already been torn down — not by force, but by trust. A kind of trust Scarlet hadn't known she was capable of giving. She'd always believed her strength came from control, from keeping her heart sealed off like classified intel. But Boris had never asked her to be vulnerable. He'd simply waited — silent, patient — until she allowed herself to be.

She curled into him under the torn wool blanket they'd found, not for warmth but because the shape of his body made her feel less like a fugitive and more like a human being again. The kind with feelings. Regrets. Hope. He didn't move or speak, just let her rest against him as the night grew colder. His heartbeat was slow and steady beneath her cheek, and it reminded her of all the things she thought she'd have to sacrifice to be good at this life — connection, intimacy, softness. But now, wrapped around him in the dark, she realized it was those very things that were keeping her alive.

"You think they'll ever stop chasing us?" she whispered into the space between his collarbone and jaw.

"No," he said simply. "But maybe they'll get tired of losing."

Scarlet chuckled softly. "Cocky for a man who's been shot at twice this week."

"And yet here I am," he said, tilting his head to look at her. "Still beside you."

It wasn't a declaration of love. It didn't need to be. In their world, loyalty wasn't a word you spoke — it was something you proved over and over again, usually with blood. And the kind of loyalty they'd shown each other? That was as rare as clean hands in espionage.

She wanted to freeze this moment — to tuck it away in a place the world couldn't touch. But even as she allowed herself to lean into the comfort, her brain kept working. She was a spy to the bone, trained to anticipate the next five moves before anyone made the first. They still had to deal with the aftermath. Mason Grey. The fallout from the leak. The fact that her face — and Boris's — were likely plastered across every watchlist on the continent by now.

And yet, none of that scared her as much as the thought of losing what they'd just found.

She shifted slightly, so she could see his face more clearly in the half-light. "We can't stay here. Not for long."

"I know."

"We'll have to move fast. New IDs. Back channels only. The kind of ghosts the agency doesn't even whisper about."

His lips quirked. "Sounds like a plan you've already mapped out."

Scarlet smirked. "I always do."

He reached for her hand, lacing his fingers through hers. "Then lead the way, Agent Swanson."

The words were spoken like a tease, but Scarlet caught the edge of reverence beneath them — the kind that came from someone who didn't see her as disposable or fragile, but dangerous and whole. And maybe, for the first time in her life, she believed she deserved that.

Because she was done hiding behind mission briefs and tight cover stories. She was done playing someone else's game.

From now on, the only mission that mattered… was survival. Together.

Chapter 9: The Ultimate Betrayal

Scarlet had been careful. She always was. But somewhere along the way, a slip-up—a moment of distraction—had led to her capture. The ambush had come swiftly, and despite her training, they had managed to outmaneuver her. A well-placed dart to her neck had knocked her unconscious, and when she awoke, she was already here, shackled to a cold steel chair in the dimly lit interrogation room. The sound of the door slamming shut was the first thing she heard as reality set in. She was no longer in control.

The sharp snap of the door slamming echoed through the stark white walls of the underground facility, sending a shiver down Scarlet's spine. The buzz of fluorescent lights above her buzzed like a distant hum in her ears, but she barely heard it. Her focus was on the sound of footsteps in the hall. They were coming. She knew it. They always came when you least expected it — when you were at your most vulnerable.

Her heart raced in her chest, but she refused to show it. They were coming for her because she had done the impossible. She'd broken the chain. She'd exposed them. She'd broken the trust of the very agency that had trained her to be a weapon. But in doing so, she'd finally found a purpose greater than survival. It was freedom. A freedom she hadn't realized she needed until it had been threatened, and now, she was paying the price.

The door swung open with a harsh screech, and two men entered. One was a familiar face — a man she once trusted, back when she had believed in something more than the game. **James Rhoades**. He was once a mentor, a figure who had guided her early in her career, teaching her the intricacies of espionage and how to survive in the shadows. They had worked together on several operations, relying on each other, even sharing moments of camaraderie and understanding in the cold world they inhabited. But that was before the betrayal.

His dark eyes were cold now, his face hard. The years had not been kind to him, and the betrayal was clear in his posture. Scarlet hadn't expected to see him here—certainly not like this.

"Scarlet," Rhoades said, his voice tight, controlled. He stood in front of her, eyes scanning her face, as though looking for any trace of weakness. "You've made your choice."

She didn't flinch. "I've made the right choice," she said, her voice steady despite the pounding of her heart. "You're the one who's made the wrong one."

Rhoades's lips twisted into a bitter smile, though it didn't reach his eyes. "You think you're the hero here? You think exposing us to the world makes you some kind of martyr?"

"No," she said, meeting his gaze. "It makes me someone who finally saw the truth. Something you're too afraid to face."

Rhoades's eyes hardened. "You betrayed your country. You betrayed the very people who trained you. People who trusted you."

Scarlet's chest tightened at his words, but she refused to let it show. The betrayal wasn't hers. It was his — it was theirs. They had turned their backs on the truth, and they had buried it beneath layers of lies. She wouldn't back down now.

"You've been part of something bigger than all of us, and you sold us out," Rhoades continued. "You were good, Scarlet. You were loyal. You had a future here." His voice softened for a moment, almost like a memory slipping through the cracks. "But you chose him."

Scarlet didn't flinch. "And I'll choose him again, every time."

Rhoades stepped forward, his hands clenched into fists. The air between them thickened. "You think he's going to save you? You think he's going to walk through that door and pull you out of this? Because he's not. He's not coming, Scarlet. No one is. You're on your own now."

Just as he said it, the room went silent. The unmistakable sound of footsteps reached her ears — slow, deliberate. The air shifted. She knew those steps. She would recognize them anywhere.

The door to the room creaked open again.

There, in the doorway, stood Boris.

His presence was enough to send a shock of recognition through her. He was real. He was here. In the flesh. Not a shadow in her mind, but standing there, muscles tense, eyes burning with the intensity of a man willing to burn the world for what he cared about. For her.

He stood tall, unmoving, his gaze locked on Rhoades. His jaw tightened, and the room seemed to shrink under the weight of the tension between them. Scarlet's pulse surged, and a rush of emotion flooded her — fear, relief, and a deep, undeniable sense of connection. He was here. He had come for her, as he always had.

Rhoades stiffened at the sight of him. "You're making a mistake, Boris," he said, voice cold. "You know what this means. You know you'll be branded a traitor too. It's over."

Boris didn't speak. Instead, his eyes flicked to Scarlet for just a moment — a brief, silent exchange that spoke volumes. It wasn't about words. It was about the bond between them. The trust, the sacrifice. They didn't need to say anything.

Boris's hand twitched toward his gun, but he didn't pull it out. His fingers brushed the edge of the holster as if weighing the consequences of what would happen next. He wasn't looking for violence, but if it came, he would be ready.

"I'm not here to fight," Boris said quietly, his voice calm but steady. "I'm here to take her."

"You're making a mistake," Rhoades repeated, but his voice cracked this time, and the uncertainty was there — a hint of vulnerability, buried beneath his hardened exterior.

Boris's gaze remained steady. "No. You made the mistake the moment you decided to sell her out. You took everything from her, and now I'm taking her back."

Rhoades took a step forward, his face inches from Boris's. Scarlet felt the tension in the room, the potential for violence hanging in the air. Rhoades wasn't backing down. He couldn't. Not without losing everything he had ever believed in. But Boris stood firm. He wasn't backing down either. This wasn't about fear. It wasn't about the job. It was about love.

"I won't let you take her," Rhoades said, his voice low but dangerous.

Boris didn't flinch. "You don't have a choice."

The moment seemed to stretch for an eternity. But it wasn't Boris's gun that won the standoff. It wasn't the physical confrontation. It was the truth. The undeniable truth that Scarlet knew all too well. They had no more loyalty to this life. No more allegiance to the shadows they had once served.

She tried to stand from the chair, defiance in every movement. "I don't belong to you, Rhoades," she said, her voice cutting through the tension in the room. "And I don't belong to this. I've seen enough of what you've done. The lies. The manipulation. It ends here."

She looked directly at Boris, her heart racing with the truth she'd buried for so long. "He's right. We don't have a choice."

And for the first time, the agency was the one that had been backed into a corner.

In the end, it wasn't about violence. It was about standing together. They weren't just fighting for their survival anymore. They were fighting for redemption. Fighting for the future they could still carve out, despite everything that had been taken from them.

Rhoades looked between them, eyes filled with a mixture of anger and disbelief. He couldn't comprehend what they were doing. He couldn't understand how they could walk away from it all — the life they'd built, the sacrifices made. But Scarlet didn't need him to understand.

"You've made your choice," Rhoades said, his voice now tinged with the defeat of a man who had lost everything.

Scarlet nodded, her resolve unwavering. "And so have you."

Rhoades stared at her for a moment that stretched far too long, as though he were trying to peel back her skin and see what remained of the woman who once followed orders without question. But that woman was gone. The woman who had served the agency without hesitation was buried beneath years of betrayal, subterfuge, and manipulation. She had once been a tool in their hands, a weapon molded to follow their commands without ever questioning the morality of those commands. But now, she was something more — a force of her own, unbroken, unapologetic, and filled with a quiet fury that burned beneath her calm exterior.

"You don't know what you're up against," Rhoades said, his voice sharp with frustration, yet there was an underlying fear that he couldn't mask. "The whole agency's hunting you now. You think you can just walk away from all of this? You think Boris can just swoop in and save you?"

Boris didn't move, his hand still hovering near the gun holster, his eyes never leaving Rhoades. "I'm not here to save anyone, Rhoades," he said with chilling clarity. "I'm here because this is where I belong. And where she belongs, too."

Scarlet took a slow breath, her mind racing through the consequences of what she had just said. She had made her choice, and now she had to live with it. She could feel the tension in her muscles, the tremor in her fingertips, but she fought to keep her composure. Rhoades wasn't just a former colleague. He wasn't some nameless bureaucrat who had chosen the wrong side of history. He was someone she had trusted. Someone she had looked to for leadership. And now he was standing across from her, eyes hard with the resolve of a man who had sold his soul to keep the wheels of the machine turning.

"You've already crossed that line," Scarlet said, stepping closer to Rhoades, her voice steady and unwavering. "You made your choice the moment you sided with the people who lied to us. The moment you chose the system over the truth. You are Mason Grey." Scarlet realized having unmasked his alias."

Rhoades's lips curled into a tight, humorless smile. "The truth? Is that what you think this is about? You've been living in a fantasy world, Scarlet. There's no truth in espionage. There's no honor. There's only survival, and in survival, you sacrifice everything." He leaned in slightly, his eyes narrowing. "I thought you understood that. I thought you were one of us."

"I was," she said softly, her gaze never leaving his. "But then I woke up."

Boris watched the exchange quietly, his eyes scanning Rhoades's every move. He knew this wasn't about the physical confrontation. This was about breaking Rhoades mentally, shattering his worldview. The mission was over. Now, it was a matter of survival. And survival meant understanding the enemy. Understanding Rhoades. Scarlet had already done that.

"The people we trusted," Boris said, his voice cutting through the tension, "they don't care about us. They never did. They use us, manipulate us, and when we've outlived our usefulness, they discard us like trash."

Rhoades's jaw tightened, and his fists clenched. The words hit home. He knew it as well as they did. It was the bitter truth that no one wanted to face, but it was the reality they all lived in. Scarlet had known it, had felt it like a cold hand around her throat, for years. But it had taken this — this ultimate betrayal — for her to finally break free of the chains that had held her.

Scarlet stepped forward, her voice now low and firm, carrying the weight of all her years in the field. "If you think you're still doing the right thing, Rhoades, then why do you look so damn miserable? You've been lying to yourself for too long. But I'm not going to pretend anymore. And neither is Boris."

The sound of approaching footsteps — the telltale rhythm of more guards — broke the moment. Rhoades stiffened, a flicker of panic crossing his face. He didn't want this confrontation. He hadn't expected it to escalate this far. He thought they could be bought, manipulated, forced back into the fold. But here they were — defying him, defying the agency, and shattering the walls of the world they had all once belonged to.

"They're coming," Rhoades hissed, his voice sharp with urgency. "You don't have time for this. You think you're going to just waltz out of here with him?" His eyes flicked to Boris, then back to Scarlet. "You'll never escape."

For a split second, Rhoades's eyes darted toward the door, calculating his next move. The tension in the room was palpable, as thick as the smoke before a storm. He knew the only way to stop them was to break their resolve, to push them into a corner where they had no choice but to surrender. He knew, deep down, that if they left that room, if they made it out alive, they would be a threat — to him, to the agency, to everything he had fought so hard for.

But he also knew that the clock was ticking, and soon it wouldn't matter what he wanted. The world was already turning its eyes toward them. His world, the one built on shadows, was crumbling.

Boris's voice broke through the silence. "We're leaving now, Rhoades. And you're not going to stop us."

Rhoades opened his mouth to speak, but Scarlet was already moving. With one swift motion, she pulled out a concealed knife, cutting through the bonds that held her to the chair. The speed of her movement took Rhoades off guard. He had never expected her to fight back — not like this. But she was no longer the agent he once knew. She was someone else now, someone who had learned to fight with everything she had, even when it seemed like there was no way out.

"We don't need you anymore," she said, her words cold and final. "And you can't stop us from doing what's right."

Without another word, she turned to Boris, who was already moving toward the door, his gun in hand, ready for anything. Scarlet followed, heart pounding but determined. She had made her choice. And there was no turning back.

As they stepped into the hallway, the sounds of footsteps grew louder. Guards were closing in from both ends, their voices urgent and sharp. But Scarlet and Boris were faster. They had planned for this. Every move they made was calculated, every step purposeful. They weren't going to let the past — or the agency's grip — define their future.

And as they disappeared into the dark, the sound of gunfire ringing behind them, they knew that the ultimate betrayal wasn't the one Rhoades had orchestrated. It was the one the agency had forced upon them — the betrayal of everything they had been taught to believe.

But that betrayal was now their strength. And it would carry them to the truth.

They moved swiftly through the shadows of the compound, the echoes of their footsteps muted by the heavy weight of what they were doing. Every turn, every corner they rounded, was a step further away from the lives they had known, the lives they had been forced to live. They had no illusions anymore. There was no going back to the comfort of their old identities, their previous loyalties. No neat exits, no safety nets. This was survival in its rawest form. Every decision, every moment, was a battle. But now, it was no longer just about surviving. It was about breaking the chains that had bound them for so long.

Boris's gaze was sharp, scanning the narrow hallway as they approached a security door. The air was thick with the scent of cold metal and urgency, and the silence between them felt less like tension and more like a shared understanding. He knew what this moment meant. The consequences were as real as the gun he carried, and yet, there was no hesitation in his steps. He was following Scarlet — because he trusted her. Because, in this fight for freedom, they were each other's strength.

Scarlet's heart pounded in her chest, but her focus was unwavering. The world had already been turned upside down, but it was more than just the agency and the mission now. It was them. It was their lives, their love, and the betrayal that had started this path of destruction. The man they had once believed in, Rhoades, had never seen this coming. He had never understood the depth of what they were capable of, together. And now, they would make him regret underestimating them.

They reached the door, and Boris quickly worked on the panel, bypassing the system with practiced ease. It felt like a lifetime ago when they were both operating under the same set of rules, back when the idea of defying the agency had been unthinkable. Now, here they were — on the run, but more alive than they had ever felt. The adrenaline was no longer something to fear. It was fuel. It was what kept them moving, what kept them pushing forward.

With a soft click, the door opened, and the corridor beyond was illuminated by low, flickering lights. Scarlet glanced at Boris, her hand brushing against his briefly. It was a small, almost insignificant gesture, but it was enough. It reminded her that, even in the darkest moments, they weren't alone. Not anymore. They had each other, and for the first time in a long while, that felt like everything.

As they slipped into the next hallway, the weight of their decision began to settle in, heavy on Scarlet's chest. This wasn't just a mission anymore. It was personal. They were no longer fighting for the agency's approval, for the government's twisted sense of order. They were fighting for the truth. For the right to live without fear, without the constant pressure of a life built on lies. It was liberating and terrifying all at once.

They moved faster now, the sound of distant footsteps in the corridor making them pick up the pace. They were no longer alone in this fight, but they were the ones with the most to lose. Everything hinged on their next moves. Everything depended on staying ahead, staying one step in front of the hunters who would stop at nothing to bring them back into the fold.

Scarlet's mind raced with possibilities as they reached the exit. Mason Grey now known by his real name. Rhoades was the mole. They were unsure how he gathered so much intel. They would get to the bottom of it, no matter the cost. They had no more loyalty to the system that had betrayed them. They were no longer pawns in someone else's game.

As they reached the final door, Boris stopped, his hand resting on the handle. He looked at her, his eyes locked onto hers with an intensity that sent a shiver through her. "This is it," he said, his voice low and steady. "Are you ready?"

Scarlet took a breath, her heart pounding, but her resolve was stronger than ever. She nodded. "I've never been more ready."

The door opened with a soft click, and they stepped out into the cold, night air. The world beyond the compound was quiet, almost too quiet. But there was freedom in the silence. There was the possibility of something more. Something real. The agency might be hunting them, but they would face it together. And, as they stepped into the shadows of the night, Scarlet realized that no matter what came next, this was the beginning of the rest of their lives.

They were free. And they had the power to decide how their story would end.

Chapter 10: Escape or Exile

The air felt different now, heavy with finality. The moon hung low in the sky, a thin crescent against the velvet backdrop of a world that had already moved on, indifferent to their fate. They had come a long way, too far to turn back, and yet here they stood, at the crossroads of everything they had fought for — and everything they had left behind.

The world knew them now, not as agents or operatives, but as ghosts. The lives they had once lived, the names they had worn like armor, were nothing more than distant echoes, drowned beneath the weight of the truth they had exposed. They were fugitives. Pariahs. And, for the first time, that didn't feel like a punishment. It felt like freedom.

Scarlet stood at the edge of the makeshift grave, her fingers brushing the cold stone marker as if she could reach into the earth and pull the past from its depths. The wind swept through the deserted field, carrying with it the scent of damp soil and something far more final. Behind her, the small boat bobbed gently in the water, a silent reminder of the escape that lay ahead. The horizon beyond was dark, the waves silent as they lapped against the shore. This was the last step, the final act. The world would believe they were dead.

"I should've learned to swim," Scarlet said softly, her words almost lost in the wind, a small attempt to bring some levity to the heavy silence between them. But her smile didn't reach her eyes. It was just a mask. A distraction.

Boris stood next to her, silent, watching the small memorial they had built together. The act of faking their deaths wasn't as simple as it had seemed in theory. It required meticulous planning, an understanding of how the system worked, how the agency would move, and how quickly they could slip through the cracks. The boat was just the final stage — the part where they disappeared into the night, the last trace of their former lives erased.

"I'll teach you, if you ever decide to return to the world," he said, his voice gravelly but warm, as if there were still something alive between them. He hadn't let go of the dream. He hadn't let go of her. And she hadn't let go of him.

Scarlet turned toward him, meeting his eyes. There were no more secrets between them, no more lies. Just the raw honesty of the moment, the unspoken truth that had held them together through everything. They had escaped together, they had fought together, and now, they would live the rest of their lives together. In this final chapter, there was no mission. No more war. Only them.

They had chosen to fake their deaths, not just to escape the agency, but to escape the war within themselves. To shed the skin of the people they had been, the people who had lived on the edge of betrayal, survival, and sacrifice. It wasn't just about surviving this life. It was about leaving it behind completely.

Scarlet's eyes drifted back to the boat. She could already imagine it — the waves carrying them away from everything they had known, into the unknown. There was a strange comfort in that thought, a sort of relief that she hadn't expected to feel. But the more she thought about it, the more she realized: they were never going to get away from who they were. The scars would never fade, the memories never completely erased. But it didn't matter anymore. They weren't running from the past. They were running toward something. Toward each other.

"Are you ready?" Boris asked, breaking the silence. His voice was soft, steady, but there was a quiet urgency there. They had planned for this, but now that the moment was here, the weight of it pressed against them like the gravity of an approaching storm.

Scarlet nodded, the finality of the moment settling in her bones. "I am."

She took one last look at the grave, her fingers brushing the stone marker one more time. There was no going back from this. The people they had been, the lives they had lived, were buried here. They were no more.

"We made it, didn't we?" she whispered, almost to herself. She wasn't sure who she was asking. Maybe it was just the question that had plagued her all along. Had they really made it? Was this the right choice?

Boris's hand rested on her shoulder, grounding her in the present. "We did. And we will keep making it, every day. Together."

The words were simple, but they held the weight of everything they had been through. The betrayal. The lies. The heartache. The moments when they had almost given up. But they hadn't. They were here now, and that was all that mattered.

Together, they walked to the boat, their steps steady. The engine rumbled to life, and as the boat began to glide through the water, Scarlet looked back at the land, at the world that had defined them for so long. It was fading now, slipping behind them like the last remnants of a dream, and all that remained was the open sea. The unknown.

As the shoreline disappeared into the night, a strange sense of peace settled over her. This wasn't the end. It couldn't be. She and Boris had chosen this path, this life. They had made the decision to leave everything behind, to fake their deaths and disappear into the world. But they hadn't just escaped. They had chosen each other. They had chosen a future. It was the ultimate act of defiance, the ultimate act of love.

"No more missions," Scarlet said softly, her voice a quiet promise that was both final and freeing. "No more war. Just us."

Boris's smile was soft, but it carried the weight of a man who had seen the worst of the world and was now ready to see something better. He squeezed her hand, his voice low, filled with the certainty of someone who had made peace with their past.

"Just us," he echoed.

As the boat carried them further from the life they had known, the future seemed wide open, the stars ahead of them infinite. There was no way to know what awaited them, but for the first time in a long time, neither of them felt afraid.

The mission was over. The war was done.

And now, it was just them. Together, facing whatever came next. And that, Scarlet realized, was enough.

As the boat surged through the cold waters, Scarlet leaned back against the side, her gaze fixed on the dark horizon. The endless sea stretched before them, a vast, empty expanse that symbolized both freedom and uncertainty. She had never been one to romanticize the unknown, but for the first time in years, the unknown didn't feel like a threat. It felt like a chance. A chance to rebuild, to redefine what her life could be. A life without shadows hanging over her every move. A life without the constant tension, the weight of missions, the burdens of espionage.

Beside her, Boris sat with his back straight, his eyes scanning the water, his mind likely working through the same tangled mess of thoughts. She knew him well enough to sense it. He was a man who rarely rested, always thinking ahead, always strategizing. But now, in this moment, there was a subtle shift in him too. He wasn't thinking about the past or the next mission. He wasn't thinking about their survival. For once, his thoughts were on something simpler — something he hadn't allowed himself to think about for years: a future. Their future.

A soft breeze kissed her skin, and the cold stung, but she welcomed it. It was cleansing. It stripped away the last traces of who she had been and what she had been taught to believe. There was no agency now. No handlers. No missions. No expectations. She was just Scarlet, and for the first time in her life, she was free to define that however she chose.

Her mind drifted back to the moment when she had decided — truly decided — to break from the agency. It had been the ultimate act of rebellion, an act that had come with a price she hadn't fully understood until that moment in Rhoades's office. But there had been no hesitation then. No lingering doubt. She had seen the truth, and with it, she had made a choice. It had been the only choice, and now, as the boat cut through the water, she was finally beginning to understand just how deep that choice ran. It wasn't just about escaping her past; it was about embracing the possibility of something new. Something that wasn't defined by anyone else but her and Boris.

Boris' voice broke through her thoughts, steady and low. "We don't have to do this alone. Not anymore. You've been carrying this weight for so long, but we've got each other now. And that's all we need."

Scarlet's heart fluttered at his words, the sincerity in his voice filling the space between them. She had never allowed herself to believe in something so simple before. She had spent so many years focusing on the mission, on survival, that she had forgotten how to connect with the parts of her that yearned for love, for intimacy. But as the words settled in her chest, she realized that they weren't just words. They were the promise of a life they would build together, outside of everything they had once known. And that promise was the strongest foundation they could have hoped for.

She turned her head to look at him, her eyes soft, filled with unspoken words. There was so much she wanted to say to him, but for once, words seemed unnecessary. Instead, she leaned toward him, the quiet trust between them speaking louder than any declaration could. His eyes met hers, and for a brief, fleeting moment, there was nothing but the two of them. No past, no baggage, no agency, no war. Just them.

A flicker of something passed across Boris's face. Maybe it was doubt, maybe it was uncertainty — but there was something else, too. A recognition. The way their fingers brushed together, a delicate touch that spoke volumes. She could feel the hesitation in his hand, as though he were unsure if he had the right to take that step, if he was allowed to finally reach out and take her hand. But that was the thing about them, wasn't it? They had both been broken and remade so many times that this moment — this fragile peace — felt like a fragile gift they were afraid to unwrap too quickly.

But Scarlet wasn't afraid. Not anymore.

She reached for his hand, her fingers intertwining with his. It was simple, but it was everything. She didn't need to say the words; she had already shown him. They were doing this together. They were choosing each other, choosing to step into this unknown with no guarantees and no safety net.

"The boat's not the end," Scarlet said softly, her voice barely a whisper, as though saying it out loud would make it more real. "It's just the beginning. We still have everything ahead of us, Boris."

Boris squeezed her hand in return, a small smile tugging at the corners of his lips. "And we'll face it together. No more looking over our shoulders. No more shadows. No more lies."

It was a promise, one she didn't need him to repeat. She had already seen it in his eyes, in the way his hand had tightened around hers. The air between them had changed. It was no longer thick with the weight of their decisions. It was lighter now, like the breath of fresh air after a long storm. The worst was behind them. The agency, the betrayals, the endless nights spent running from their own shadows — it was all fading. And all that remained was them, together, on the cusp of something new.

For the first time in years, Scarlet felt the weight lift from her shoulders. The past no longer defined her. It had shaped her, yes, but it didn't control her anymore. There was no more being a pawn in someone else's game. No more playing by their rules. She was free to build something from the ground up, something that was uniquely hers and Boris's. And for the first time in her life, that felt like everything.

Boris turned to her fully now, his face inches from hers. His breath mingled with hers, the promise of their future in the silent space between their lips. "Whatever comes next," he said, his voice low and filled with determination, "we'll face it together. Just us."

The words hung between them, not as a question but as a declaration. There was no turning back. And for Scarlet, that was the only certainty she needed.

The boat cut through the water, carving a path toward the unknown. But for once, that wasn't something to fear. It was something to embrace. They had chosen this path. Together. And whatever it held, they would face it as one.

As the boat glided across the water, Scarlet allowed herself to close her eyes for a moment, listening to the gentle lapping of the waves against the hull. She could feel the cool breeze against her skin, a reminder that the world was still moving on — still turning. But for the first time in years, the world outside felt irrelevant. The noise, the chaos, the ever-present danger of the life they had left behind were now nothing more than distant memories, fading with every mile they put between themselves and the shadows they had lived in.

She opened her eyes to find Boris still beside her, his gaze fixed on the horizon, his expression unreadable. But she knew him better than that. She knew the strength it took for him to be here, to allow himself this — this chance, this hope. He had spent so many years keeping his walls up, not allowing anyone to see the cracks in his armor. But now, she was the one who had helped him tear them down, just as he had done for her. The vulnerability they had shared, the trust they had built, was everything. It was something neither of them could have imagined a few months ago, and yet, here they were, together. Choosing each other. Choosing life.

"Do you ever wonder what happens now?" Scarlet asked softly, the question hanging in the air between them. It wasn't fear or doubt that laced her words, but a simple curiosity. The future was so wide open now, so filled with possibilities. She wasn't looking for answers; she just needed to acknowledge the enormity of what they had done. It wasn't just an escape; it was a rebirth. A chance to create something entirely new.

Boris turned to her, his eyes meeting hers with a quiet intensity. "What happens next is up to us," he replied, his voice steady, unwavering. "The rest of the world might never understand what we've done, but it doesn't matter anymore. We've chosen this life.

Together. And whatever comes, we'll face it together. There's no one else I'd want by my side."

Scarlet felt a lump form in her throat, the raw emotion of his words catching her off guard. They had both fought so hard for so long, lived in a world of lies and deception. And now, they were finally free. Free to make choices that didn't involve survival or loyalty to anyone but each other. They had chosen love. They had chosen to let go of the past and build something new. She squeezed his hand, her heart swelling with a love that, despite everything, felt endless, boundless.

The boat continued to move across the open sea, the darkness enveloping them as the last remnants of their past lives slipped further behind. There would be no more missions. No more lies. Just the two of them, charting their own course into an uncertain, yet promising future. And for the first time, Scarlet wasn't afraid. Because in Boris, she had found her home. In the chaos of their world, amidst the shadows they had escaped from, they had built something real. And no matter what came next, they would face it, together.